Dear Reader,

Welcome to our exciting showcase series for 1997!

Harlequin Romance books just keep getting better—and we enjoy bringing you the best choice of wonderful romance novels each month. Now, for a whole year, we'll be highlighting a particular author in our monthly selections—a specially chosen title we know you're going to want to enjoy again and again....

Simply the Best: *authors you'll treasure, books you'll want to keep!*

We start the New Year with popular author Eva Rutland. Then look out next month for *Marry Me* by Heather Allison...especially for Valentine's Day!

Happy Reading!

The Editors

Eva Rutland began writing when her four children, now all successful professionals, were growing up. Eva lives in California with her husband, Bill, who actively supports and encourages her writing career.

If you've ever daydreamed about giving up your day job and finding a rich, gorgeous husband to keep you in luxury...we know you'll love this book! Eva Rutland treats us to a humorous look at life as her heroine, Lisa, sets herself up as *Marriage Bait*.

Also, look out for the follow-up story...coming soon in Harlequin Romance.

Don't miss any of our special offers. Write to us at the following address for information on our newest releases.

Harlequin Reader Service
U.S.: 3010 Walden Ave., P.O. Box 1325, Buffalo, NY 14269
Canadian: P.O. Box 609, Fort Erie, Ont. L2A 5X3

Marriage Bait
Eva Rutland

Harlequin Books

TORONTO • NEW YORK • LONDON
AMSTERDAM • PARIS • SYDNEY • HAMBURG
STOCKHOLM • ATHENS • TOKYO • MILAN
MADRID • WARSAW • BUDAPEST • AUCKLAND

If you purchased this book without a cover you should be aware that this book is stolen property. It was reported as "unsold and destroyed" to the publisher, and neither the author nor the publisher has received any payment for this "stripped book."

ISBN 0-373-03439-3

MARRIAGE BAIT

First North American Publication 1997.

Copyright © 1997 by Eva Rutland.

All rights reserved. Except for use in any review, the reproduction or utilization of this work in whole or in part in any form by any electronic, mechanical or other means, now known or hereafter invented, including xerography, photocopying and recording, or in any information storage or retrieval system, is forbidden without the written permission of the publisher, Harlequin Enterprises Limited, 225 Duncan Mill Road, Don Mills, Ontario, Canada M3B 3K9.

All characters in this book have no existence outside the imagination of the author and have no relation whatsoever to anyone bearing the same name or names. They are not even distantly inspired by any individual known or unknown to the author, and all incidents are pure invention.

This edition published by arrangement with Harlequin Books S.A.

® and TM are trademarks of the publisher. Trademarks indicated with ® are registered in the United States Patent and Trademark Office, the Canadian Trade Marks Office and in other countries.

Printed in U.S.A.

CHAPTER ONE

"GOOD morning, Mr. Harding!" Lisa Wilson's voice had a cheerful ring which gave the day a lift, even when it was riddled with a dozen baffling decisions and even if she was just saying, as she was now, "Here's your coffee."

"Thank you." Scot Harding took a sip of the hot brew with a dab of cream and no sugar. Another thing he liked about her. Like the coffee, she, with evident enjoyment, voluntarily took on several tasks not to be expected of today's women employees. None of which had anything to do with his decision. He chuckled to himself. It was going to blow her mind when he told her. "Sit down, Lisa, I've something to tell you."

Lisa didn't hear him. She was addressing the broad-leafed rubber plant that graced his luxurious office. "Oh, my, you're a little thirsty, aren't you, dear?" she questioned as she poked a finger into its soil.

"Never mind that," he said a little sharply. She would have to discard some of those domestic habits, as well as those skirts and loafers she favored. Smarten up a bit. "There's something I'd like to discuss with you. Sit down, please."

5

Lisa looked surprised, but obediently took the chair beside his desk.

"You know, of course, that Sam Elliot deserted us for Enterprise Limited."

"Yes." He shouldn't have been surprised. Enterprise had been courting Sam for six months.

"Rather precipitously and at a most inopportune time," he said. "Leaving me in a bit of a spot."

"Yes." Everyone connected with the insurance firm of Safetech International knew that Scot Harding, Vice President in Charge of Operations, was seeking a replacement for his administrative assistant. And everyone, especially here at Corporate Headquarters in Wilmington, Delaware, was vying for the coveted position, a shoo-in for executive director or vice president of one of the prestigious regions like Paris or London. Or, as Sam had opted for, a promotional transfer to another firm.

As Harding stood before her, listing the requirements for the post, which she already knew, Lisa idly wondered who he had in mind. Maybe Stanford in Fiscal, or Jenkins, from Property and Casualty. But bets were high among the staff that this time it would be a woman. If that were so, it was sure to be Reba Morris. Sue Jacobs, her secretary, was pretty sure Morris was sleeping with him. Possible, Lisa thought. Even the austere Ms. Morris would be tempted, if not eager. Not only was he way up there in the Safetech hierarchy, he was young, not quite thirty, and yes, good-looking, she thought, studying him as he, still talking, paced back and forth behind his desk. He was tall with the lean muscular figure of an athlete. His thick black hair had a tendency to curl and was always unruly, at variance with his perfect attire, the most expensive of imported Italian business suits, complemented by everything that went with them. His face? Yes, it could be handsome...in spite of that serious intense look. If he would just relax, laugh more. All business. She wondered if he ever took the time to sleep with anyone.

Suddenly she was aware of the quiet. He was looking at her. Expecting her to say something. What?

"I...I beg your pardon," she said.

He smiled. The sweet, rather boyish smile transformed his whole face. A pity it was so rare. "I don't wonder that you're surprised," he said. "But you can handle it."

"Handle it?"

"Sure you can. You have often worked with Sam. In some cases, covered for him."

It took her a minute to grasp it. He was offering her Sam's job. Good grief!

"But I don't..." She stopped. Not polite to say she didn't want it. "I don't...don't think it would be right. I do appreciate the offer. But I couldn't . . . shouldn't take it on.''

He couldn't believe this. Was she turning it down? A position so far above her present one that it . . . well, it was inconceivable. Never mind that he had been hesitant about offering it to her. She was only twenty-three, had been with the firm only two years, and in the lowly capacity of secretary to his personal secretary, Celestine Rodgers. But he had observed her competence. And now . . . Perhaps he had misunderstood. "What exactly are you saying, Ms. Wilson?"

"That . . . I couldn't. I do appreciate the offer, but his position . . . it's just not for me.''

"What do you mean, it's not for you?'' He was unable to mask his irritation. "I've seen you take over, both for Celes when she had one of her migraines, and for Sam, during several of his unexplained absences. And pretty damned efficiently, I'd say.''

"That was temporary.'' She seemed to be begging him to understand. "It would be unfair of me to take such a demanding job on a regular basis. I don't have the time.''

She meant it. Her eyes, her best feature, open, guileless, and utterly revealing, never concealed anything. She wasn't being coy or trying to negotiate for better terms. Damn! She hadn't even asked about money. She didn't want the job. No time.

"What the hell . . . I mean, what is keeping you so busy?"

"Getting married."

"Oh." He was relieved. "That should pose no problem. I'm sure we could arrange time off for such a momentous occasion. When is the wedding?"

A wary look flashed in those dark blue eyes before long, concealing lashes brushed her cheek. "I . . . I'm not sure."

"I see." Probably marrying some chauvinist who objected to a working wife. Hadn't caught up with the twentieth century. Or was afraid her salary would outdistance his own . . . which it probably would. He wondered . . . "Who's the lucky guy?"

She got up quickly, not looking at him. "I . . . haven't decided. I'm sorry, Mr. Harding, but I'd better get back to my desk. Ms. Rodgers will be looking for me." She muttered other phrases. "Appreciate your thinking of me . . ." and "Sorry" before making her escape, but he was too stunned to listen. She hadn't decided? That was a hell of an answer. How many offers did she have?

He shrugged. Never could tell, could you? Couldn't tell by looks, anyway. Well . . . startling eyes. Too big for that pixie face though. Her shoulder-length hair was a mousy brown. She was too short and a wee bit too plump for his taste. But some men . . .

Hell! Why was he thinking about her? The Paris conference coming up. And that controversy over the new casualty law. He needed an assistant like yesterday. One who knew what happened last month. Like Lisa.

Oh, well. Stanford. Fiscal would collapse without him.

Jenkins. Too ambitious. Like Sam, he'd be gone before he could be any real use.

Damn. Another reason he'd chosen Lisa. Not only was she not ambitious, she was too young and naive to be snapped up by the competition. By the time they spotted her assets. . . .

Hell. Forget her. No use fooling with someone who doesn't want the job. And someone tied up with some chauvinist who'd not want her to leave town or . . . Tied up with more than one evidently. Funny, he'd never have thought . . . Oh, he guessed she was attractive enough, but a long way from a number ten. Not the type to be overrun with suitors.

Lisa gave her desk drawer a vicious slam. So she had lied!

"Something wrong, dear?"

"Oh. No, nothing." She glanced across the room to give Celestine Rodgers a reassuring smile. "Just banged my hand a bit." She took the stack of papers from her In basket. She hadn't exactly lied. She was getting married . . . as soon as she found a man she wanted to marry. And convinced him to want to marry her, she thought, smothering a chuckle as she switched on her computer.

Anyway, if she had lied, it was his fault. Why hadn't he just said "Okay, sorry" to her "No, thank you" instead of standing and gaping like he was God Almighty who had just offered this snip of a girl the moon and stars and the stupid idiot was turning it down.

Darn right she was turning it down! Taking that job would be like a mouse biting into a morsel of appetizing cheese, once tasted, hard to resist. And she was not about to be sucked into the butt-kissing, corporate-ladder-climbing rat race. She had seen enough of it in the person of her Aunt Ruth, who had coiffured, kicked, and clawed her way to the very pinnacle of success in the banking arena. And what had it got her! A gold watch and a lonely, loveless, companionless, childless, frustrated retirement.

At one time Lisa had felt at fault. But, no. Ruth was in her mid-forties and already committed to the corporate life-style when her five-year-old orphaned grand-niece was dumped into her lap.

No, it wasn't quite true, Lisa thought, grinning. She would have slid off that sleek slender lap if

Ruth had ever been around long enough for her to climb into it. Which she wasn't. Too busy staying sleek, slender, well-groomed and perfectly coiffed. Too busy being tops in her position and making the right impression or connection to mount the next rung on the banking ladder.

Not that Lisa blamed her. It must have been most inconvenient for Ruth Simmons, single and in the midst of a flourishing career, to be suddenly saddled with a young kid. But, without a word of complaint, Ruth had assumed the role of guardian.

Guardian angel, really, for that was how Lisa always thought of her. An angel, hovering somewhere in the distance, with a fat checkbook, magnificent gifts of toys, clothes, and dancing lessons, peppered with occasional perfumed weekend visits to her apartment, or trips to the theater. Ruth had supplied the money and the glamour, but she had assigned the mothering to Mary Wells.

So it was Mary Wells into whose lap Lisa had climbed when she scraped her knee or was teased by one of Mary's three boys. It was Mary who soothed, comforted and, on a few occasions, spanked her bottom. It was Mary who had been beside her for Halloween trick-or-treating, selling Girl Scout cookies, sitting on the bleachers at Little League games, sharing the picnics and potlucks at school and other youth functions. Love and laughter still reigned at the Wells household, and Mary's eyes still twinkle with happiness when she quietly plays pinochle with her now-retired husband or attends a game or potluck with one of her young grandchildren.

As Lisa's fingers expertly skimmed the computer keys, her mind reinforced her resolution. To have the solid family life that Mary Wells had, but with a bit of the glamour touched upon with Ruth...the opera, travel, advantages for the children, not possible on Mary's thin budget. She would have to find a husband who could afford both.

Nice work if you can get it!

Well, darn it, she could try, couldn't she?

When Lisa entered the employee's lounge at noon, the discussion was going at full blast as several lower echelon employees debated over whose boss or boss's boss would get what. Principal, at the moment was the coveted A.A. to Harding.

"It's bound to be a minority." Alice, from Legal, stopped polishing her glasses to look up at Lisa. "You're on the inside, Lisa. Who do you think? Stanford?"

Lisa shrugged. "Could be." But doubtful, she thought, sliding in beside Sue and unwrapping her chicken sandwich. Stanford was African

American, and too smart for his own good. Who could replace him at Fiscal?

"It's certain to be a woman this time," Sue said decisively. "This morning—"

"Ha!" Stu, one of the two males present, broke in. "Beats me how you can term yourselves a minority! We've got women execs coming out of our ears!"

"Nevertheless," Sue continued. "This morning Ms. Morris was urgently summoned by Mr. Harding, wasn't she, Lisa? Did you see her?"

Lisa nodded. She had seen her, all right, the picture of professional elegance, sucking up to Ms. Rodgers, which wasn't a bad idea. Harding had a tendency to listen to his long-time secretary.

Sue's smile was smug. "She didn't say anything when she came back, but I have a feeling..."

"Feelings!" Stu scoffed. "This is a business and Harding is no fool. He'll pick someone who's competent and reliable, and knows the business from A to Z. Now this guy in properties..."

The talk went on and on, but Lisa didn't listen. She placed her tape recorder on the table and stuck the small earphone into her ear, munched her sandwich and listened to the fluent French phrases. When she traveled with her husband to foreign countries, she meant to have some knowledge of each language.

CHAPTER TWO

HARDING was exasperated. Women! He had thought Reba Morris would solve the minority problem and perhaps work out as a fairly suitable assistant.

He was wrong. He had spotted that come-on look the minute she walked into his office this morning. Definitely a danger signal. Office liaisons could interfere with business, and he was wary of women who thought they might sleep their way to the top.

Damn! He knew his quest for a woman assistant would evoke erotic ideas in the minds of a few harebrained idiots. He just had not expected Reba Morris to be one of them. But that look. That touch, casual but seductive, as she bent forward in a wave of exotic perfume to remove a bit of lint, probably imaginary, from his coat. Oh, she had some enticing assets, he had to admit. But not the ones required, and the fact that she thought it necessary to advertise them might mean that she was not as keen businesswise as he had thought. Anyway, it was evident that her austerity was a facade; one of her several faces.

No, Ms. Morris was out. Maybe he'd have to seek further afield. That guy from Dallas that had impressed him at the conference—

His buzzer sounded and he picked it up. "Hal Stanford is here, Mr. Harding. He'd like—"

"Send him in." He rubbed his chin. Stanford. Maybe, after all . . .

"Hi, chief. How's it going?" Hal Stanford, a tall, brown-skinned man, came in carrying a sheaf of papers. "Thought I'd better go over these figures with you before I release them."

"Sure." Harding stood up and walked around his desk. "I'm glad you're here, Stan. I'd like to sound you out about something."

"Oh?"

"You know I'm seeking an assistant. How would you like—"

Strong white teeth flashed against dark skin as Stanford, grinning, shook his head. "Please, Mr. Harding, I don't want to go," he said with a smile.

"Jeez!" Scot stared at him. "You, too?"

"What do you mean . . . me, too?"

"I mean, you're the second person who's turned down what I thought was a most desirable job. Even before I offered it to you. Hell. What's wrong with me?"

"It's not you, boss. It's the travel."

"Travel?"

"Yep." Stanford nodded. "You do keep your A.A. hopping all over the globe."

"Well, what's wrong with a little travel?"

"Leaving home," said Stan. "Not only my lovely wife, but the three kids who keep us both jumping."

"I see." He looked at Stanford as if seeing him for the first time. He knew he was quick, efficient. Hadn't known he was such a family man.

"Thanks for the offer. I do appreciate it, but...well, Hal Junior is just starting Little League and...well, I'd kinda like to be around. Maybe when the kids are older..." Stan shrugged. "Anyway, take a look. What do you think?" He spread the papers on the desk and the two men bent over the figures.

Later, when Stanford departed, Scot Harding was thoughtful. Strange how the first two persons approached—the ones he had decided most capable for the job—were too involved to be interested. One in being married, the other in getting married.

Strange. He had never thought much of this marriage business himself. His mother had died when he was five, and his father had been interested in nothing but his brokerage firm. Scot and his brother, Chuck, spent precious little time at the family estate, and were always glad to get away from the passel of servants and back to their boarding school, or, during vacation, to some camp.

Back to the swimming, tennis, or golf and other games. It had been fun. Exhilarating. He liked the competition, the challenge. Just as he liked it now in the businessworld. That was why he had decided against joining the family firm, and had sold his share to Chuck. The brokerage business was a guessing game, dependent upon the rise or fall of various markets. Scot liked having his own hand in the outcome, getting ahead of the other fellow by offering the best idea or package. Competition. He hadn't exactly started at the bottom at Safetech...could he help it if his father had friends? But the fact that he was moving up rapidly was the result of his own initiative and skill. As exhilarating as a hard set of tennis.

As for marriage... Hell, Chuck's two mishaps were prime examples for avoiding it. He smiled, thinking of his brother, about to make a third try with a certain redhead. But that was Chuck...staking everything in a guessing game.

All of which has nothing to do with my present problem! Scot threw his pencil on the desk and walked to the window. Who would be his best bet?

During the following week he conducted several interviews, even making a hurried trip to talk with the Dallas prospect. He made no offers, just sounded out each candidate.

Sounded out and found wanting. Damn!

The trouble, he finally admitted, was that he had already made up his mind. Lisa Wilson was his best possible choice. His first apprehensions about her youth and inexperience had been entirely erased by her refusal of his offer. Now she represented a challenge. Scot Harding did not shirk from a challenge.

Perhaps a dinner engagement with Lisa and the prospective groom. He'd never seen a guy, chauvinist or not, who could not be influenced by money. He'd casually bring up the job offer again, mentioning the salary. It would help if he could first check out the man, his prospects and financial situation. Lisa hadn't mentioned a name, but...

Hadn't decided? Surely he'd misunderstood. He would get Celes on it right away.

He was about to ring for her when his own buzzer sounded. "Ms. Morris, Mr. Harding."

Damn. Not again!

It was not in Lisa's nature to be envious, but she felt a certain lack, a vague yearning, as, for the fourth time in three days, she watched Reba Morris disappear into the chief's office. Tall and willowy. The best I can achieve, Lisa thought, is short, okay, average, and shapely. Shapely, that is, if I lose about fifteen pounds. And how, she wondered, did the exotic Ms. Morris maintain that look of smooth, everything-in-place perfection, everything, that is, except one enticing curl escaping from that luxurious sweep of silky black hair. A neat trick. That businesslike sleek combined with a dose of something... Sexy? Sensuous? Whatever, I could use some, Lisa thought. I wish it came in a can.

She sighed. Maybe she had started at the wrong end. All that reading of great books and opera, studying foreign languages, gourmet cooking, and golf. All the things that would make her the versatile well-rounded woman, the perfect wife for the kind of husband she wanted. If you wanted everything, you had to be everything.

However, to be a wife, one had to get married. The trouble was that men, most of them, went for the package, never giving a thought to what it contained. Look at George Wells, married to a fluff of a blonde who didn't know beans about caring for children, nor would she dare muss her hair by joining him in a game of softball, two of George's basic requirements.

And, Lisa thought, I'm aiming higher than a George Wells. If I'm to compete for a high-caliber male in a world where women outnumber men ten to one, I've got to be more than ready. I've got to be beautiful!

She sighed. Easier said than done. For a moment she wished her aunt Ruth wasn't on one of her interminable cruises. No. Ruth would be busy advising her to take Harding's job offer. She was on her own.

It was that night that she saw the ad. Sitting at the kitchen table in her little apartment, munching at a salad and trying not to think of the cookies on the top shelf of the cabinet, she thumbed through the latest issue of *Women*. A full-page ad in the middle of the magazine jumped out at her. "A New You. Get a complete makeover at Hera's Beauty Spa. Hera is the Goddess of Women and Beauty, and that's what we're all about. All. Fitness and fashion, as well as the basic beauty treatments. Why shop around when everything you need is here?"

Excitement bubbled through her. Not exactly a can, but about as close as she could come.

The very next day, Lisa did what the ad advised, made an appointment with one of their beauty counselors. She was surprised that she could be seen that very evening, also that the facility was within walking distance of the office. Convenient.

The salon was located on the first floor of a modest building and the discreet, gold-lettered Hera's on the entry door gave no indication of the opulence within. Lisa became apprehensive as soon as she entered the reception area. Everything about it, plush carpet, potted palms, elegant furnishings, even the decor of quiet turquoise, screamed "Money!" She was a little short of that item. Maybe she should...

"Oh, yes, Ms. Wilson." The chic young woman in a black sheath and pearls looked up from her French Provincial desk and smiled. "Loraine will be with you momentarily. Do have a seat."

Lisa sank into one of the cushioned sofas, feeling distinctly out of place in the setting. She exchanged a smile and nod with an overweight woman with stringy blond hair who sat across from her. You and me, she thought. It will take a miracle.

A miracle you have to work for, she realized later as she was shown behind the quiet elegance to a beehive of activity. Women of all shapes and sizes lifting weights in the exercise room, soaking in the mud baths, being pummeled on the massage tables. There was the beauty parlor with its miracle-making hair, facial, and makeup techniques. There were the nutrition and fashion consultants who gave personal counseling. And when she was shown the before and after pictures, her heart pounded with eagerness to get started.

But the miracle must be paid for, she was told, when at last she faced Loraine in her private office. Five thousand dollars, payable in advance.

Lisa choked. She had thought in terms of small monthly payments.

Loraine smiled. "Impossible. Perhaps you can arrange a bank loan?"

Celestine Rodgers looked at her boss in astonishment. "Getting married? Lisa hasn't mentioned any such thing to me."

"Well, she mentioned it to me," Scot said. "Find out who the guy is. I want a dossier on him."

Celes, still looking mystified, shook her head. "I had no idea. A wedding. Perhaps that's why she's getting this loan."

That got his attention. "Loan?"

"Yes. Personnel sent over this form. Seems the bank must have assurance of tenure of employment before granting—"

"How much?"

"Five thousand." Again she shook her head. "These young people. All this to make a big splash for one day, when it could go toward a down payment on a house. It's like I told my niece—"

"Have you sent that form back?" Scot asked.

"Form?"

"For the loan."

"No. But I have signed it and—"

"Bring it to me." Scot realized his secretary was looking rather curious. "Interest rates. Banks can often take advantage," he added quickly. "I'd like to take a look at it."

"Of course," she said. "And I'll find out about her fiancé right away."

"Never mind," he said. "In fact, I'd rather you didn't mention it. Awkward, since she hasn't said anything to you." Maybe he wouldn't have to bother with the fiancé, he thought. If Lisa needs money... Money, the great persuader.

He waited until the end of the day to summon her. He would need time with no interruptions. When Lisa faced him, he didn't waste words. He shook the loan paper at her. "Do you know how much you're borrowing?"

Lisa wondered how it had come to his attention, but answered steadily, "Five thousand dollars."

"No, my dear. You're borrowing almost twice that much."

"No. Only five thousand."

"Compounded by fourteen percent interest for a period of..." He looked down at the application, then back at her. "Yes, indeed, stretched out like this, you're paying for considerably more than you're getting."

"Oh." She hadn't thought of that. Still... she needed it. "I can manage two hundred a month. Not five thousand all at once," she said, her voice crisp. It wasn't his concern.

"I see." He gave her a speculative look. "Perhaps something could be arranged. I presume you want this for your wedding."

"Wedding?" What was he talking about?

His gaze sharpened. "You are getting married, aren't you?"

"Getting...?" She stopped, remembering. "Yes. No..." Not easy to lie. "That is, not exactly."

"What do you mean, not exactly? You're either getting married or you're not."

"All right! I'm not." Her eyes burned into his. Not his business!

"So why did you lie?"

"I didn't lie."

"You certainly did. You said you were too busy because you were getting married."

"Because you kept pushing!"

"Pushing?"

"Shoving me into a job I didn't want."

"No way! If you didn't want the darn job, all you had to do was say so."

"I did! But you had to have a reason, sir," she snapped. Lisa had held her own against three tough Wells brothers too long to let herself be bullied by any man, boss or not. "And I did not lie. I did not say I was busy because I was getting married. I said I was busy getting married."

He stared at her. "There's a difference?"

"There certainly is. A person can get married or a person can prepare to do so. I'm preparing."

"I see." He didn't. She could tell he was trying to figure it out. "Let me get this straight. Actually, you are not getting married. You are just preparing to do so."

She nodded.

"With, I suppose, a certain someone in mind."

"Not . . . not exactly."

The lift of his eyebrow was more than a question. It was a command.

"A . . . a certain type," she said haltingly.

"A type?" He looked so bewildered that she almost laughed. But then he frowned, leaning toward her. "I wish you'd make this clear to me. You are getting married . . . no . . . preparing to marry . . . not a certain person, but a certain type of person?"

"And what's wrong with that?" She wanted to slap that grin off his face!

"Nothing. Nothing at all," he conceded, still looking amused. "A type . . . Let's see. Tall, dark, and handsome? Blue-eyed blonde? Or . . . big, iron-pumping bozo with bulging muscles? Or—?"

"Sir, you are being rude. If that is all, Mr. Harding . . ." She stood, poised to leave.

"Come now. Don't get upset." He changed his tone and gently motioned her back to the chair. "I'm trying to understand. You are not interested in appearance, but . . . Let's see . . . rich man, poor man, beggar—"

She stood up again in utter disgust and moved toward the door. "Sir, I've had enough. May I leave?"

He caught her before she reached the door, held it and condescendingly said, "Wait. I'm sorry. Calm down. I really am interested. What type of man are you looking...preparing to—"

"Not your type," she said, gulped, and gave a wry smile. "No offense, sir. I promise you he won't be so involved in work that he doesn't have time to enjoy a marriage. And he'll earn enough so that I can stay home and enjoy it, too. And we'll have children, and we'll travel, and we'll have fun."

The bewildered look had never left his face as she talked. Now he spoke almost jovially. "Sounds like he'll have to be independently wealthy and retired to come up to your standards."

She hadn't aimed that high, but... "Maybe," she said. "If we're to do a lot of traveling."

The woman was serious.

Heck, what else was new? Most women were aiming for marriage, weren't they? And preferably to a rich man.

But most were not this direct. In the first place, they wouldn't admit it. And they sure wouldn't turn down a promotion like this...not while the hoped-for bird was still off in some vague bush, anyway.

"Come, Lisa, let's sit down and talk this over." He led her back to the chair. "You're working now, aren't you?"

She nodded.

"So why couldn't you take a job in the same place that pays you more money and—"

She shook her head. "Too demanding and I don't want to get caught in the corporate rat race like...like some people."

"All right." He tried another tact. "When you meet this paragon...and, for the moment, we won't delve into where or how you'll find him...has it occurred to you that he might not have the same...er...inclinations?"

Her eyes flashed. "Why do you think I want the loan?"

His lips twitched. "To incline him?"

"Exactly."

"Whoever or wherever he is."

"You make it sound like—"

"An exercise in futility, which it certainly is. Whatever induced you to be sidetracked into such a ruse when you could be pursuing a profitable and rewarding career?"

"I am pursuing a career. Marriage."

"Marriage is a union between, I might remind you, two people."

"Well, it's usually the woman who makes the marriage. So I consider it her profession. The oldest for women, I believe, except for prostitution."

Somewhere deep in the all-business heart of Scot Harding trickled a murmur of old-fashioned romance which rankled at the idea of marriage and prostitution in the same category. Still . . . the way Chuck's ex-wives were taking him did have the taint of prostitution. One reason he intended to avoid the so-called sacred institution of marriage. Some treated it as some kind of con game.

He glared at Lisa. "This is a deliberate, cold-blooded scheme to entrap some man you don't even know."

"Well, yes."

He winced at the blatant admission. "It's not right, all this plotting and preparation."

"People go through much more to achieve a promotion in business."

"That's different."

"No, it isn't. As I said, marriage is an occupation, a rewarding one that makes a contribution more valuable than money."

"Maybe. If it's the right kind."

She stiffened. "Why do you think I'm planning so carefully? I assure you that mine will be the right kind, Mr. Harding. I'll be able to stay home with my children, for one thing. Do you know how many children are neglected because nobody is at home or nobody cares?"

"Don't get off the track. You are deliberately setting yourself up as bait to catch any unsuspecting guy in your trap!" The woman was crazy. And why, in this day of women's liberation, was he saddled with a woman who just wanted to get married? Which would be all right with him if he wasn't convinced that she was his best prospect for—

"Will that be all, Mr. Harding?" Lisa stood, poised to depart.

"Just a moment." She might be crazy, but she was open, guileless. Unlike Reba, no facade. One face, frank and honest.

No raving beauty, either. And since she was so picky about the right man... Yes, indeed, this marriage would likely be a long time coming.

"Sit down, Ms. Wilson. We might be able to reach some compatible agreement."

CHAPTER THREE

IN THE exercise room of Hera's salon, Lisa lifted and stretched, stretched and lifted with dutiful precision, but her mind was at Safetech, editing the list of people Harding had selected for the Paris conference.

"Look this over," he had said. "And make sure I've not left any key people out."

Her name was among the rest. A conciliatory gesture, she thought. Because, to be honest, there was very little she could contribute. On the contrary, a great deal she would learn.

Was that why she had been included?

No. Not the only reason, anyway. He'd been making sure the staff knew, and was exposed to his new man—woman. His duly qualified and authorized stand-in, the Administrative Assistant, i.e., Chief of Staff.

She greatly appreciated his support. But she was not ready to go to Paris. Not ready in more ways than one.

How could she make him understand without harm to her status or his?

"What's this?" He had sounded irritated. "You've scratched your name. We made an agreement."

"No good unless I get my part of the bargain," she had answered.

"You did. Five thousand dollars."

"But it's not the money," she argued. "It's what the money paid for."

"So. You paid. What's keeping you here?"

"Packaging," she said, unable to stifle a smile. "You see, it takes time to—" She broke off. It was not funny to him. "I'm jesting," she said quickly. Darn! Hadn't she learned from Mary Wells that the best way to get what you wanted from a man was to make him think that was exactly what he wanted? "My real concern is your part of the bargain."

"Oh?" He looked suspicious.

"It's a big jump from a gopher to an administrator," she said, trying to look more helpless than she felt. "You trusted me to make that jump, Mr. Harding, and I appreciate it. I want to be a good assistant for you."

"Oh, you will be. I am confident that you will. And you'd best begin by calling me Scot."

"Thank you, Mr....Scot," she said meekly. "But seriously, sir, don't you think, that to be really effective, it's important that I also gain the confidence of your staff?"

"Of course."

"You know that will take time. There may even be one or two who feel . . . well, slighted." Reba Morris, for sure, she thought, watching his reaction.

He frowned. "Perhaps. But business is business, and—"

"And, as you say, a smoothly running business is dependent upon a happy and cooperative staff," she finished. "You see, Mr. Harding—I mean, Scot. Oh, shucks, it's going to take me some time to get used to this first-name status." He smiled, waving off her concern, and she continued, albeit a little awkwardly. "I was about to say that, since my appointment I've heard through the grapevine, rumbles of discontent. Mainly Ms. Morris. So I put her in my slot."

"Reba?" That got to him. Was it the conception among the staff that Reba had been passed over...perhaps unfairly? Well, hell! Reba may be competent, but she has her own personal agenda. One that is competitive to business and damned uncomfortable for me. No problem with Lisa in that regard. She'll make a great A.A., a company man . . . only needing a little technical improvement, which will come in time. "Reba?" he said again.

Uh-oh, Lisa thought, noting his quizzicality as he repeated her name. Maybe I've gone too far. She tried to interpret his expression. Guilt? Was he really sleeping with Reba and had . . . Not my business, she decided, and quickly added, "The Paris caper is really important for the company to win," she said, feeling her way. "Ms. Morris knows the foreign portfolio as well as anybody in the firm. And what's more, her presence being required will dismiss the rumor that she was passed over."

Scot took a long breath. Nodded. "It makes sense. Okay. I think you're right."

Lisa was relieved. "Thanks, Mr. . . . Scot," she said. "Then I can remain and get a better handle on things here . . . really stand in while you're away."

Scot chuckled. "Case closed," he said. "Just check the list carefully, will you?"

She knew that Scot, loaded with other responsibilities, had depended on her predecessor to audit these kinds of selections. She determined to be sure he had the right combination. The most reliable group, those with whom he would feel most comfortable.

She knew that Scot always wanted his exec with him on such missions, and she meant to accompany him. Later, when she would be an asset, to herself as well as to him. She recognized that one of the pluses in her new job was the opportunity for foreign travel, to the most likely places to find a rich and retired potential husband. But not yet. Not until she had made herself into the right package to attract such a man. Well, as right as she could make it. She really didn't expect a miracle. She'd have to make up the lack with charm. No problem, she thought with a wry smile. Any girl who could charm George Wells into escorting her to the junior/senior prom... Now, at least she didn't have the challenge of braces and acne.

So, on with as much miracle as she could get. She was lucky that the salon was in the vicinity, within easy access after work. She found the exercises invigorating and the nutrient supplements and recommended diet extremely effective. She had already lost five pounds, and never felt hungry.

"Have you finished with these weights?" Ada asked. Ada was the stringy-haired blonde who had sat across from her that first evening. It looked as if she had lost weight, too.

"Sure. Here you are." Lisa handed over the weights, and made her way through the mass of perspiring women to the showers.

After a quick shower, Lisa sat in a mud bath, thinking about the agreement made with Harding. Not a bad decision. An interest-free loan from the company, allegedly for accepting the position as his assistant. Not bad at all. With her raise in salary, she could pay off the loan in a few months. And she had found that giving orders was far easier than taking orders and running like a chicken with your head off to carry them out. No longer was she typing out agenda after agenda, faring out or receiving urgently faxed messages, and making interminable phone calls to track down some important person somewhere. She was sitting in her own pleasant office, recently vacated by Sam, his leftover secretary at her command. She was making decisions and discussing policy with Scot, or quietly conversing by phone with the important individual someone else had tracked down. She had spent hours on the phone with the Paris executive, discussing the bid package details and schedules. Everything would be set for the conference, as soon as she notified and conferred with the company participants. A task Scot had assigned to her. Another attempt, she strongly suspected, to increase her exposure as his assistant.

She scheduled the meeting. She felt extremely nervous as she surveyed the people at the table, all more experienced than she, all doubtful of her. Perhaps it was Reba Morris's smug watcher-her-fall-on-her-face expression that saved her. She wasn't all that inexperienced. Hadn't she pulled Sam out of a hole more than once? And . . . well, darn it, didn't charm work in business, too? She took a deep breath, and, assuming an air of casual confidence, opened the meeting.

"You all know, perhaps better than I," she said, "how important this particular conference is for our European connections. That is why the boss has limited attendance, he told me, to his old pros. You are all seasoned and tenured. No Johnny-come-latelies.'' She pointed to herself and smiled. ''So I'll run the ball for you here at the head house. If you need anything, just yell.'' The downplay of her position worked well. All smiled agreeably and delved into the agenda talk and logistics with vigor. With good humor and some respect for the new A.A., she thought, and breathed a sigh of relief.

On a Saturday morning three weeks later, Lisa stood in her apartment and listened to the rain pounding against the windows. A good day to work inside. She looked with satisfaction at the papers scattered on her bed. Not scattered, darn it. Pretty well organized. She had been right to bring all this East African business home with her. It was not yet easy for her to deal with personnel and company position papers for the exec at the same time.

Not doing too badly though, she thought as she continued to sort the material. At least she was managing pretty well with personnel. Just plain graciousness, which came natural to her; please, thank you, and would you mind, combined with a few what-do-you-think or how can we handle this or that? And of course she had been lavish with praise for the key people who had returned triumphant from Paris. Even Reba Morris had softened up and was now, oh, so helpful, if still a bit condescending.

Now, if she could get a better handle on corporate policies. This East African venture was awesome. Safetech had been expanding so rapidly in Uganda that, more than a year ago, plans had been completed for the erection of a ten-story Safetech building in Kampala, its capital. The plans had had to be shelved because of political problems, but now they were up and running again. Data had come in detailing all aspects of the project, which she was now in the process of cataloging and highlighting for Scot. He had not been in the office since he'd left for Paris, having detoured to several regional offices…Stockholm, Berlin and London. He was to make a report on the Ugandan project to the board on Tuesday, and she wanted to have it ready for him. It was just one of several important issues she was organizing for his easy perusal. His modus operandi was to be on top of whatever was happening right from the first, so she always faxed important data to him, wherever he was. He was too hyper, so tense and anxious about nothing but business. And, darn it, she was getting to be one of these corporate types herself, trying to keep up with him. Working this weekend when she should be at the salon. But she knew he'd be in Monday and she had to have this ready.

She was making good headway when her doorbell sounded. Darn. Probably the paper boy. She got off her knees and went to answer.

Clarice stood there, looking somehow smarter than usual, even in her dripping raincoat. She was holding Todd, the baby, and three-year-old Betsy was still pressing the doorbell.

"Oh. Clarice!" Aware that she sounded anything but welcoming, Lisa quickly changed her tone. "Hi! How nice. Do come in," she said, all the while thinking this was bad timing. "Come here, Todd, give Lisa a big hug."

Clarice handed the baby to her, and turned, calling over her shoulder. "I'll just get the diaper bag. Be right back."

Diaper bag? How long were they staying? Lisa wondered as she, still holding on to Todd, took off Betsy's slicker and tried to unravel what she was saying. By the time she had deciphered "I'm hungry. I want a Popsicle," Clarice was back.

"Okay, here's everything, diapers, bottle, and two jars of baby food. Sure, a Popsicle's okay. They usually have a snack about this time. Oh, and here's a box of crayons. Just give Betsy some plain paper and that'll keep her busy for a while." Before Lisa could speak, Clarice had dumped the diaper bag and other paraphernalia, and was off again, saying she should be back later. "Thanks, Lisa. You saved my life today. So sweet of you to volunteer to baby-sit."

Volunteer? Oh, good heavens, she had. Last Saturday at Mary's! "Sure, Betsy. You can have a Popsicle...I think." Lisa, struggling with Todd's jacket, tried to remember if she still had Popsicles in the fridge, while she retraced her visit with Mary Wells.

She went often to visit Mary. It was so peaceful, sitting on the patio, helping Mary shell peas and admiring her garden.

But, last Saturday, when she'd stepped through Mary's garden gate after her session at the salon, she found the place in an uproar. Both children were yelling, and Mary, holding baby Todd in one arm was trying to reach a fast-retreating Betsy.

"Lisa! Thank God." Mary thrust Todd into her arms. "Here. I've got to get those clippers away from Betsy."

It wasn't funny, but Lisa was hard put to keep from laughing as she surveyed the disaster. Every one of Mary's prize roses, neatly clipped, was scattered on the ground, a howling Betsy, cowering behind a rosebush, trying to escape her distraught grandmother.

Mary wrested the clippers from the child, but vented her rage upon her mother. "That Clarice!" she exclaimed, the expression which always indicated her denunciation of the woman, George, her youngest boy and prized baby, had married. "She ought to be looking after her own children. But she's out finding herself!" Mary's voice rang with sarcasm. "A pity she didn't start looking before she married my George barely out of high school."

Lisa settled Todd in the playpen with her car keys, and enticed the still sobbing Betsy to help her collect the roses. "We should never cut Grandma's flowers unless she tells us to do so. But maybe if we collect these and arrange them in a vase, she won't be too upset."

That didn't help, Lisa thought now as she searched in the fridge for Popsicles. Mary had continued to rail against her daughter-in-law. "Do you know what she did? Went to some placement seminar to be tested for her right career. I told her she already had one. Why when I was a girl, all we wanted to do was get married. I belonged to this club...we called it the WGM... Supposed to be a secret, but that stood for Wanta Get Married, which we all did. We weren't ashamed, either, cause it wasn't a disgrace like it is nowadays. Seems like all the young mothers today have a need to get out of the homemaker closet to do their own thing. Whatever that is. And while that Clarice is looking, I'm stuck with her kids and I'm too old for this!"

Clarice painted a different picture, Lisa thought as she told Betsy to "Stay in the kitchen until you finish your Popsicle." She placed Todd on the kitchen floor with his, constructing a barricade with two kitchen chairs.

"Mary just doesn't like me," Clarice had said. She had returned for the kids and Lisa was helping her load them into her van. "And she's wrong. I do love my kids. But how would you like to listen to baby talk twenty-four hours a day? Twenty-four!" she exclaimed when Lisa gave her a skeptical look. "I'm practically a single mother, you know, with George driving that big rig all over the country. And when he is home, his idea of recreation is for me and the kids to watch him play softball with his team. Big deal!"

Sounds like George, Lisa thought. But he needs the exercise after fighting highway traffic for several days.

"Can't you see why I was going stir crazy?"

"Yes," Lisa sympathized as she'd strapped a squirming Todd into his car seat.

"Well, I said to myself, there must be more to life than this. So I went to this placement seminar." Clarice's eyes sparkled...just like they had when she was homecoming queen. "The lady said I was a natural techie. That's the term they use to say a person's good at technology," she explained. "They say that I could easily adapt to any computer program technology, and that major companies are clamoring for that kind of skill. So I'm going to this training school every Saturday and it's absolutely fascinating."

Lisa didn't have the heart to tell her that punching computer keys could be as dull as baby talk. Anything that could bring back that much sparkle... But it was as much to relieve Mary as for Clarice that she'd offered to baby-sit. And for George. She did owe him. He'd not only taken her to that long-ago prom, he had bullied some of his football buddies into dancing with her.

And, despite the mess, she was enjoying the children. By the time the kids finished with what didn't land on them or the floor, the baby was sleepy. Holding him on her shoulder, she rocked back and forth on the sofa, at the same time entertaining Betsy with fairy tales. Yes, I do want children, she told herself, feeling the sweet warmth of the baby snuggled against her, and watching the fascinated eyes of Betsy as she listened to what the baby bear said. She was glad she had promised to baby-sit. This was part of preparing, too, wasn't it? she thought as she settled the sleeping baby on a blanket on the living room floor, and cleared the coffee table for Betsy's papers and crayons.

Two hours later, they were sitting at the kitchen table, Betsy munching a peanut butter and jelly sandwich while she fed Todd, when the doorbell rang. Holding Todd carefully in front of her in order not to get his food on herself, with Betsy trailing behind, she went to answer.

"Thank God you're here," Scot said. "I thought maybe you'd gone somewhere and left your phone off the hook." His where-did-they-come-from look focused on the kids. "Are these yours?"

"Today they are," she answered. "Just until four, I hope."

"Oh." Still looking puzzled, he said, "Where did you put the Ugandan data? I've been looking everywhere for it."

CHAPTER FOUR

"I THOUGHT... You're not due back till Monday," she said, almost accusingly as she backed away to let him enter.

"I said I'd be in the office Monday." He stepped inside, feeling somewhat amused. His A.A. looked anything but efficient. Hair disheveled, something gooey on her nose, and trying hard to hold on to that squirming baby. He couldn't help laughing. "You seem to...er...have your hands full."

"Which seems to afford you a deal of enjoyment," she said, her smile not quite hiding her irritation.

"I guess it's the sight of you in a different role, and..." He stopped. The sight of her always gave him a lift, no matter what she was doing.

She hadn't heard him. She was reaching for the little girl. "No, no, Betsy!"

Too late. A sticky hand tugged at his raincoat. "Hi."

"Why, hello, young lady." He bent down to face a pretty little girl with peanut butter and jelly smeared on her face. "What's your name?"

"Betsy. Do you got any candy?"

"No, he doesn't have any candy, and it's not polite to ask. Now, you've said hello very nicely, Betsy. Why don't you go back into the kitchen and finish your lunch while Mr. Harding and I..." She ended on an inquisitive note, glancing at him.

"Oh." He stood up. "The Uganda data. I couldn't find it, and I couldn't get through to you on the phone."

"Oh." She glanced toward a phone which lay on the floor...disconnected. "I'm sorry. One of the kids must have been playing with it."

"That's okay. Just tell me where the Uganda material is and I'll get out of your hair."

"It's here. I knew your report is on the agenda for Tuesday's board meeting, and I thought... Well, I was going over it for you. Digging out the pertinent facts, but..."

"Don't apologize for heaven's sake. That's great. I haven't had a chance to tell you, but I sure like the way you operate. It's not easy to keep on top of things when you're jaunting all over the globe. Your concise messages, cleared of the garbage, really saved me time. And kept me abreast." He inclined his head. "Glad to have you aboard, lady."

"Thank you," she said, but looked a little dubious. "I'm afraid I don't have it quite ready, and..." She broke off, drowned by the baby, who, he thought, sure had a pair of healthy lungs.

"He's hungry," Betsy, who hadn't moved, explained.

"Feed him," he said to Lisa. "I'll get it. Where is it?"

She glanced uncertainly toward a closed door. "It's not...not ready," he thought she said.

Lord, the child was screaming bloody murder. "Feed him! I'll find it," he said, and went across the room and opened the door. He stopped. No trouble finding it. It was spread all over the damn bed. At least he guessed this was it. He strode to the bed and picked up one of the papers. "Political policies of the Ugandan government greatly influence the economy and..." That was it, all right. He glanced about the room, breathing in that light but tantalizing odor, fresh and sweet, that he had begun to associate with Lisa. Some flimsy things on a chair, a couple of slippers askew on the floor, dusting powder on the dresser.

And papers...papers concerning the most important international caper Safetech was to pull this year, scattered carelessly, perilously...on a slightly rumpled bed!

"I'm sorry," he heard her say, and turned to see that she and Betsy had followed him in. She had shifted the baby to her shoulder and was trying to soothe him while explaining over his cries, "I...I haven't quite finished."

"I can see that." His mouth twisted. He nodded toward the bed. "This, I take it, is where you dig out the pertinent data for those concise messages you fax to me?"

"Well, it was the only place here big enough to spread it out!"

"Oh?"

"For your information, there's a lot of impertinent junk that needs digging out, and since it just came in I brought it home with me to...to..." She wasn't exactly yelling, just trying to make herself heard above the brat's screams. "I spread it out to sift it for you." She lowered her voice, shifted the baby, rubbed her cheek against his. "I know," she said soothingly, "I'll feed you in a minute."

He started to gather papers. At least it wasn't all over the floor. "Okay, I'll just—"

"Don't touch it," she said, raising her voice again. "I've got it arranged just right and I'll give it to you as soon as I feed him!"

She was right. No way could he get it together. He took off his raincoat and threw it across the chair with the flimsy underthings. "So start sifting. Give me the brat," he said, lifting the baby from her. "Shut up, you. It's coming. Where's his food?"

"I'll show you," Betsy volunteered, and took his hand to lead him into the kitchen.

Lisa followed, protesting. "You can't feed him."

"Sure I can. What's to it?" He seated himself at the table and positioned the brat on his knee. "You stick this little spoon into this little jar, fill, and poke same into this little mouth. Open up, kid."

Betsy grinned at him. "That's right. That's the way."

She might have spoken too soon. He cursed as the now silent but discriminating Todd promptly spat, much of the rejected spoonful landing on Scot's spotless shirt.

"He doesn't like spinach," Betsy explained. "You have to mix it with the peaches."

"Why, thank you, Miss Betsy. We'll try it your way," Scot said, and laughed as the baby swallowed. "Fooled you, didn't we? You've got a smart sister, kid." Looking up, he saw Lisa dubiously watching. "Well, what are you waiting for? I thought you were going to take care of business."

"I am," she said, and quickly returned to the bedroom. But the sight of Scot Harding with Todd on his knee, dribbling all over him, had been disconcerting. In fact his presence in her apartment, especially at this particular time was disconcerting. If he had called ... If her phone hadn't been off the hook ... If he had waited until Monday ...

She would have had it ready, everything in a nutshell, which he could have quickly scanned and grasped. He was good at that.

Anyway, it wouldn't take long. She had already sorted it out. Just had to separate the categories, make a few notes.

It took her longer than she thought. She was distracted by sounds from the other room, Betsy's chatter, Scot's deep laugh, even the short silences.

When she emerged about an hour later, she found all three of them on the living room floor. Todd was happily banging on several tinfoil pans, and Betsy, holding a ring of keys, was proudly telling an attentive Scot which key was which. "This one is to your car. This is to your condo... No, no... to your locker at the club, and this one..."

Lisa couldn't believe it. It was so uncharacteristic. Scot, calm and patient... even looking contented and interested. With two kids! At the office, he would be—

"Finished?" he asked, standing up. "Let me have it," he said, moving toward her.

Presto-chango, the boss was back! Might as well be in the office, she thought, as he reached for the papers in his usual impatient, demanding let's-get-this-done-and-get-it-done-right manner.

He scanned the material hastily, and she was about to explain how she had separated the different aspects when Clarice arrived. A good thing, for they were making no headway on account of the children. Even so, their departure took some doing, what with Clarice trying to gather up everything, while her inquisitive eyes focused on Lisa in silent admonition. "You never told me your boss was a hunk, not to mention that he comes a calling. Ho, ho, ho."

Scot, holding both the baby and diaper bag, escorted Clarice to the van and helped strap in the kids, during the still steadily pouring rain. When he returned, running a hand through his wet hair, she apologized, "I'm sorry. I've put you through a rather hard day."

"An interesting one," he said, grinning. "And that's what you're aiming for, huh?"

"What?" she asked, puzzled.

"What your friend...what's her name... Clarice has." He shook his head. "Not much of a picnic, carting kids and all their junk all over the place."

"Oh." She smiled. "I assure you, Mr. Harding, that when I have kids, it will not be necessary for me to cart them and all their junk to a baby-sitter."

He held up a hand. "Pardon. Forgot. You'll have a built-in nanny, what with your rich and retired banker or whatever husband."

"Exactly." She nodded, her eyes twinkling.

"Well, you better choose carefully, lady. Can't have him too retired."

"Oh?"

"Might be too old to make babies."

"Oh, you!" She couldn't help laughing at his signifying expression which somehow balanced between a question and a leer. "I thank you for the advice. I'll certainly take your views under consideration. And now for your business, sir. I've separated the categories, but—" She hesitated, looking down at the papers in her hand. "I made a few notes on each one that you probably won't understand."

"Let's see," he said, taking the package from her and glancing at the top page. "'Quo'...'tr'... Right. I don't understand."

"Notes to myself. I planned to dictate to Doris and have her type it up all neatly for you on Monday. But now...oh, it shouldn't take long for me to explain it to you. Only..." She looked toward her messy dinette table. "Just let me clear this off so we'll have room."

"Wait. It has been a long day, and I've missed lunch. Why don't I take you out for a bite first. Then I'll be in a better state to absorb all this stuff."

She glanced out the window, then down at herself. "Look, it's still raining, and by the time I got dressed ... I've got a better idea. Why don't I fix a snack and we can work while we eat."

He looked wary. "I am not in the mood for peanut butter sandwiches."

"My dear sir, we have an extensive bill of fare," she said with a smug nod. "Selections guaranteed to delight a wide range of culinary appetites."

"You don't say?"

"Oh, yes." She wrinkled her nose. "From a two-year-old peanut and jelly fan to a senior citizen retiree with a delicate constitution."

"Is that a crack?" he called as she retreated to the kitchen.

"Don't get touchy, Mr. Harding," she called back. "You could never be mistaken for a retiree. You're a workaholic."

He chuckled and shed his raincoat yet again. She had made the decision, he thought, and followed her into the kitchen.

She had already cleaned off the table and was fast putting the place in order. He laid the papers on the table, but his eyes stayed on her. He liked watching her. Even when she looked a mess, as she did now. Scuffed loafers, jeans and pullover streaked with baby food, no makeup and that mousy-brown hair bunched on top of her head. He wondered why the unkempt look made her seem untouched and vulnerable. And...yes, downright appealing, he thought with some surprise.

"This won't take long," she promised. With evident disregard for her appearance, she gave the counter a hasty wipe and began to pull things out of the fridge. "Look at my notes and check what you don't understand."

He didn't look at the notes. He couldn't stop watching her make lunch as quickly and efficiently as she handled routine office matters. With the same cheerful ease. And in the same organized disorganized fashion, he thought, remembering the papers lined on her bed.

And with excellent results, he conceded as a tasty repast was set before him. He wasn't sure what kind of soup, but he knew it was homemade, savory, well-seasoned, and thick with crisp, tasty vegetables. Not a deli sandwich, for he had watched her assemble it...chicken salad with lettuce, tomatoes, thin, toasted rye bread.

She sat in front of him, bit into her sandwich, and immediately plunged into business. "'Quo'...well, not exactly a quota, but one of the requirements is that we hire a certain percentage of their civilians. Seems fair, don't you think? Anyway, the 'tr'...we'll have to provide training for they're sure to need it." Rapidly she went through the various categories, deciphering her notes. By the time she finished, he was thoroughly familiar with the pertinent aspects of the Uganda project, political as well as economic.

"Lady, you are something else," he said. "I thought I would have to spend all day tomorrow digging out the facts you have so carefully laid out for me."

"We do our best, sir." She dimpled as she set a steaming mug of coffee before him.

Funny, he had never before noticed that dimple in the corner of her mouth. He sipped his coffee slowly, not wanting to leave. Not sure why. He had just got back, tired from a hardworking globe-trotting agenda, and irritated at having to track down the Uganda stuff. Somehow in the midst of a messy apartment with two messy brats and a very disheveled A.A., everything had fallen into place. Now he wasn't at all tired. He was alert, but relaxed in the quiet intimacy of the kitchen, the rain beating against the window, Lisa smiling at him across the table. He liked her radiant companionable smile, reflecting the teasing camaraderie that had been established between them.

"To you!" He lifted his coffee in a toast. "Before I ask, you deliver. I couldn't have a more capable, competent, far-seeing assistant."

"We try, sir, we try." She bowed her head in mock modesty, her smile widening.

His breath caught. That smile. That radiant, frank, unflirtatious smile. Open. Inviting.

On impulse he rose, walked around the table, and bent down to touch his mouth to those inviting lips. A light touch. A simple gesture of thanks. He was unprepared for the sudden warmth, an electrifying shock that made him quickly draw back. Her wide incredulous eyes returned his stare, and he knew she was just as moved, or as startled as he.

She seemed to recover first. "Watch it, boss," she said, trying to laugh, but not quite pulling it off. "That could get you sued!"

"Don't I know it," he breathed, serious. What had come over him? Never had he ever so much as touched or even flirted with a female employee. Had never believed in mixing business with...with...what was this anyway? "Look, Lisa, I'm sorry. I didn't mean anything. I just—"

"Oh, for goodness' sake, don't apologize." Now she did manage to laugh. "I know that. Guess we're both just a little cocky about getting that stuff sorted out. Some of these countries...newly emerging or with all those coups...are complicated and you get a little crazy trying to figure them out."

"Right." At the moment he was going a little crazy trying to figure himself out.

"But we did it!"

"You did it," he said. "And I'm darn grateful. My board presentation will be a breeze, thanks to you."

"We aim to please, sir," she said again, the teasing note returning to her voice.

"Good lunch, too. I owe you," he said, relieved that they were back on firm friendly ground.

CHAPTER FIVE

As THE weeks passed, Scot Harding decided Sam Elliot had done him a favor when he resigned. Lisa was the better choice. She anticipated his needs, materials appeared like magic on his desk even before he asked. She was cooperative and competent. She could be silently unobtrusive or a pleasantly official buffer between him and whomever or whatever he wished to avoid, always seeming to sense when to be which. He congratulated himself upon his good luck, and began to rely on her as upon his right arm.

One morning as he bent to search in his bottom desk drawer, he was distracted by the sight of a pair of legs. Black pumps with heels just high enough to accentuate the slender ankles and long, slender, shapely legs.

"Good morning, boss!"

His head jerked up. Lisa. He looked at the legs. Hadn't known Lisa's were that long. That shapely.

"Your coffee, sir. Better drink it while it's hot. What are you looking for?"

"The Sutter file." But now he was looking at her. She seemed slimmer and taller. Heels. No loafers.

"Oh, I knew you would want it, and put it in the credenza. I'll get it for you."

He got a good view as she walked around to the credenza. She looked pretty smart in that black coatdress, that scarf. Celes, or somebody, must have put a bug in her ear about correct office attire. Good. As she reached for the file, her dress flared apart, revealing a more extensive view of the legs encased in sheer black hosiery. Good legs, by golly! Funny, he'd never noticed.

He noticed the haircut immediately. "I like that," he said a few mornings later, when she appeared, shorn of most of that mousy-brown hair. The new short cut framed her pixie face to perfection, making the hazel eyes seem larger. And the hair was no longer mousy. A richer brown that seemed to dance with golden lights. "Is it dyed?" he asked rather hesitantly.

She grinned. "It's called frosting. And it's the final touch... the last of the packaging."

"Packaging?"

"The prettier the package, the more enticing the bait," she quipped, winking at him. Then she touched a hand to her hair, her wide eyes eager and anxious. "Do you think it makes me look... well, better?"

"Sure. Great." Too damn much better, he thought, not liking her reference to bait. Darn! Was she still on that husband-hunting kick? "All right, let me have a look at the agenda for that San Francisco conference," he said rather gruffly.

"Right here," she said, all business again. She handed the papers to him and sat beside his desk.

He tried to concentrate on the material at hand, but couldn't seem to keep his eyes off Lisa. Gad! She was quite a good-looking gal. Funny, he had never realized.

Lisa was aware, and gloated in his admiring gaze. Loraine was right! "That frosting's gonna work like a stoplight, honey! Just you wait and see," she had said. "Not a man alive will pass you without stopping for a second look."

It was happening. Lisa almost giggled. When she had asked outright, he had only grudgingly admitted that she did "look better." But now... Scot was so mesmerized by her hair that he couldn't take his eyes off it to focus on the most pressing data presently on the corporate agenda.

He liked the way she looked. She could tell. Lisa squirmed with delight, basking in the knowledge that she pleased him.

No! It wasn't him; she argued with herself. It was...well, that it was worth every penny. All the strenuous exercising, dieting, makeup. It was beginning to pay off. If the package stopped Mr.

Nothing-Before-Business Scot Harding in his tracks, what wouldn't it do to other men!

"This is major," he said rather abruptly, and she saw now that he focused on the San Francisco conference. "Earthquake insurance and governmental responsibility. We'd both better make this one."

Back to business as usual, she thought. But why did he look so...what? Puzzled? Irritated?

Both. He was puzzled by the utter enchantment at the sight of her. Irritated that he couldn't stop looking. Distracting. No place in business.

But it was some time before he began to take the new image, like the cheerful voice and perfect coffee, for granted. Later, when she accompanied him to various meetings and conferences, he saw that other men also noticed. He found himself acutely aware, and, for some strange reason, highly irritated by the many admiring glances and undue attention she received. But Lisa remained her open, businesslike, unflirtatious self, not at all receptive to any nothing-to-do-with-business advances. This relieved him and he relaxed, becoming quite proud of her. He liked having this very attractive, competent assistant sitting beside him, and quite enjoyed the envious stares of his fellow conferees.

Until San Francisco.

Lisa was glad Scot had asked her to accompany him to the conference. She had never been to California, and the meeting would be in its most exotic city. She hoped there would be time to visit Chinatown and the Top of the Mark, probably take a few tours.

At first she thought she would have no time for touring. It was a hot and heavy conference. Several insurance companies had sent key personnel, all eager to absorb the meaning of the new laws in order to formulate the most advantageous insurance packet. On the second day she ran into Sam Elliot.

"Lisa!" he exclaimed. "This can't be you."

"It certainly is," she said, chuckling. "You didn't expect me to be a gopher all my life, did you?"

"No, but..." He hesitated, his gaze scanning her dubiously. "I just didn't expect—"

"Didn't expect me to take up where you left off, did you?" she teased. "Didn't think I could take your place as chief assistant to the demanding Scot Harding, huh?"

"Oh, I knew that. Nobody knew better than I how many times you saved my skin!"

"Then, don't look so surprised, you devil. You keep looking at me as if I'd just crawled out of the woodwork."

"Oh, no, honey, not out of the woodwork... More like...Lisa, what have you done to yourself?'' He stepped back to get a clearer view. ''You're stunning, sweetheart ... positively beautiful!''

Lisa felt herself blush to the roots of her hair. No one had ever called her beautiful. And to hear it from Sam Elliot who, as she well knew, had a most discerning eye, made her feel ... well, quite beside herself. She tried to be cool. ''Flatterer! I bet you say that to all the ladies.''

''You know me better than that, my sweet. It's sure good to see you, Lisa. Let me buy you lunch for old times' sake.''

''Thanks, Sam, but...'' She glanced at her watch. ''I've got two hours before the next meeting and I plan to take advantage. I wanted to see Chinatown. Someone said it wasn't too far. Down this way?'' she asked.

''Correct. And I wouldn't dare let you go without an escort.'' He linked her arm through his. ''We'll see the sights and eat, too... at Fong Lue's. You'll like that.''

She had never seen anything like it. Lots of tiny shops as well as street stalls. Everything for sale, herbs, vegetables, and other foods, as well as many curio shops where she lingered to buy souvenirs. Throngs of people milling about. All in Western dress, but many were speaking Chinese and she was fascinated by the high crescendo of voices, the unfamiliar language with a curious singsong pitch.

They ate at Fong Lue's where Sam displayed his mastery of chopsticks, and tried to teach her.

"Never mind," she said, as the kernels of rice kept evading her efforts. "Just get me a fork."

He compromised by feeding her himself, while bringing her up to date on his doings. "I'm holding my own at Enterprise," he said. "Have to since I don't have you as a backup anymore. Say, how would you like to transfer? I could get you—"

"Stop it!" she said, laughing. "I'm already in over my head." And enjoying it far more than I ought, she thought. This travel could get to be a habit. She didn't want to get caught in the corporate race and lose sight of her goal...marriage.

She did enjoy the outing with Sam, and returned refreshed, ready to delve into business. Sam accompanied her into the session on government responsibilities in national disasters, and took his seat beside her. Scot, on her other side, greeted Sam effusively, asked about his work, and congratulated him on his evident progress.

Then he turned to her. "Where did you disappear to? I had lunch with the State Insurance Commissioner, and wanted you to join us."

"I'm sorry," she said. "I didn't know. I did a bit of touring. Chinatown."

"Alone?"

"No. Sam joined me. He took me to lunch down there. Did you know he's an expert with chopsticks? Oh, and I bought the cutest little toys for Betsy and Todd."

"Oh. Well...good," he said. But he looked anything but pleased.

When the meeting ended, Sam leaned toward her. "Hey, Lisa, there's a little supper club down near the wharf that has a great combo. Would you like to go dancing?"

"Oh, I'd love it!" she said, pushing back her chair. "Just give me an hour to change."

"All right. Let's see. It's five-thirty. I'll meet you in the lobby at—"

"Sorry, Sam," Scot broke in. "But Lisa's going to be pretty tied up tonight. Some data we've got to check out before tomorrow's session. I hope you don't mind."

"Oh. Sure. I mean...no problem. Wouldn't want to interfere with business," Sam said. His discerning look said something entirely different, Lisa thought. Like, "Wouldn't want to tread on your preserves." What on earth had given him that impression?

She was embarrassed. Puzzled. And a good deal put out!

She held her peace until Sam had disappeared into the crowd. Then she turned to Scot and spoke rather pointedly. "What data?"

He looked embarrassed. "Well, I thought we should...that is, we need to—"

"Scot! Haven't seen you since Paris. How're things going?" A stout man pushed forward to take Scot's hand.

"Lincoln. Good to see you. Have you met my assistant?" Scot said with a proprietary gesture toward Lisa.

Several other people seemed anxious to speak to him. One rather attractive blond woman suggested that he join her group for dinner. To this he pleaded business. He was cordial to everyone, genially discussing the various aspects of the session and soliciting opinions. He never failed to introduce Lisa and include her in the conversation, as if afraid she might run away.

He needn't have worried. She wasn't going anywhere until he explained. What data? It wasn't until people had dispersed and they moved together toward the elevators that she could ask.

"What the dickens were you talking about? What do we need to go over tonight?"

He cleared his throat and spoke decidedly. "Tomorrow's session is important. Governmental responsibility versus insurance claims in cases of natural disaster. I thought we should be clear about the questions we wish to bring up."

She stared at him. "We went over all that on the plane, didn't we?"

"I know. But we want to be on our toes. Alert." He hesitated, straightening his tie. "Lest you spent the entire night cavorting about, you—"

"I am not in the habit of overdoing!" Suddenly, aware that others were waiting at the elevator, she lowered her voice. "Neither am I so feeble that an evening of dancing would leave me too exhausted to..."

She broke off as they entered the elevator. It was crowded and both remained silent. But when they got off on the floor where both had rooms, she continued more pointedly. "Really, Scot, I think I am capable of spending a few hours enjoying myself in the evening and remaining alert enough the next morning to comprehend whatever business is discussed. I am not stupid. Neither am I so buried in business that I can't...can't..." Her voice broke off and she made a master effort to control herself. She was here to work, wasn't she? "Never mind! Shall we work before or after dinner?"

He was studying her intently. "It...er...maybe it's not that important. We can skip it."

"Skip it! Now? When..."

"When I've already spoiled your evening?"

She smiled. "It's just that Sam was going to take me dancing, and I—"

"You really wanted to go, didn't you?"

"Well...yes. I love to dance. And...well, it's been a long time since...oh, it doesn't matter. Really."

"All right, darn it! If you want to go dancing, we'll go dancing."

She stared at him, stunned.

"Well, don't just stand there." He nodded toward her door. "Get dressed. Sam Elliot's not the only guy who can dance, you know."

Her eyes narrowed in doubt, but resignedly she went on into her room. In the shower, she was still doubtful. She would rather have gone with Sam. Touring Chinatown with him had been fun, and when he mentioned dancing she had been overjoyed, remembering the high school years when the boys had put on tapes and the Wells's home had rocked with the feet in all the latest steps. It seemed so long ago. She sighed. Suddenly they had all grown up. The boys had all gone to work, got married, and she was busy at secretarial school and living with her aunt. Then when she went to work...well, the truth was she had never been overloaded with dates. It was like her dancing days had ended. And, this evening, when Sam had suggested dancing, it was like a door opening to fun again.

Darn Scot Harding! It wouldn't be all that important, whatever he wanted to talk about. But she knew that's what they would be doing.

Dancing? Ha! In the first place she doubted if he even knew where to go. Oh, sure, he certainly traveled as much as Sam Elliot, but, unlike Sam, Scot took the office with him.

In his own shower, Scot pondered his actions...and reactions. What was he thinking about? He had planned to spend a peaceful productive evening alone in his room, going over his brochures and notes, and drawing up a most unusual comprehensive insurance packet. After he had discussed his ideas with Lisa over a quiet dinner. She had a quick mind and a way of spotting flaws and...

That was it. Reaction. He had not wanted Sam Elliot to walk off with his prized assistant when she was here to bounce off ideas with him. He hadn't liked the look of anticipation on Sam's face, or the sparkle in Lisa's eyes as she told him about Chinatown. And when he'd found they planned to spend the whole evening dancing, it really ticked him off!

She was here to work. And, damn it, she had no right to make him feel so guilty that he was about to waste his whole evening on the dance floor. Where the devil did one go dancing in this town anyway? He picked up the phone.

Wrong. He did know where to go, Lisa thought as she was seated at the smart little supper club. Subdued lights, crisp linen, and already her feet were quietly tapping to the rhythmic beat of the combo. "Oh, this is perfect," she said, delighted that she had worn the long-waisted, short-skirted cocktail dress that looked like something out of the twenties.

"Surprised, huh?"

"No. Of course not. I just... I didn't think—"

"That I was as much on the ball as Sam Elliot?"

"Oh, no, Mr. Harding. It's just that you... your tastes run in different directions."

"Oh? How is that?"

"You know what I mean." She hesitated, disconcerted by the way he was looking at her, and not knowing how to put it. Not complimentary, either, to say Sam was too much playboy and he was too much business. "Just... different."

"I see. Well, I assure you I can handle a pair of chopsticks as well as anybody, and..." He stood, holding out his hand. "Shall we test my dancing?"

The laughter in his voice, the teasing glint in his eyes, set the tone for the evening. One of the... no, the most delightful evening she had ever spent. Different. Not one of the Wells's house-rollicking, watch-this-step routines. Not an anxious who's-going-to-ask-me-to-dance night that had spoiled her prom. No business talk, either. Silly nonsensical talk, personal, all attention centered on her. Dancing together . . . just the two of them. Had she been with anyone other than Scot Harding, or had her mind not been of such a practical nature, she might have recognized it as a romantic evening.

As it was, she simply enjoyed herself immensely. She loved dancing with him . . . light, uncomplicated steps that she found easy to follow. Liked his arms about her in that casually caressing protective way. Liked the teasing banter that developed between them.

He always watched her, enjoying the intense way she went about doing whatever had to be done. But tonight she was different, he thought, watching the pleats of that short gold skirt twirl above those perfect legs. She seemed lighthearted, carefree, wholly intent on the joy of the moment. He liked dancing with her . . . head thrown back, eyes sparkling, giving herself up to the dance in childish abandon. Well, why not? If one planned to spend a whole evening on a dance floor, might as well relax and enjoy it!

"It was a wonderful evening," Lisa said when he escorted her to her room. "Thank you, Mr. Harding. Okay . . . Scot."

"I suppose you're welcome," he said, leaning against the door and pretending to pant. "But all this prancing about does leave an old man pretty worn out."

"Oh, you! You use more energy every other day on the golf course. Probably you're suffering from all that wine. Come on in and let me revive you with a nice cold nonalcoholic soda."

He followed her in, his mouth twisted in a smile. With any other woman, that invitation would have meant more than a soda. With his guileless Lisa, it meant just what she said.

Now why did he think of her as his Lisa!

"Here's your drink, sir," she said, handing him an icy soda.

"None for you?"

"Oh, I'm in no need of reviving." She made several turns about the room, and sang in surprisingly musical tones, "I could have danced all night I could have danced...danced..."

"I believe you could," he said, chuckling as he watched her. "Lisa, you are absolutely refreshing!"

She stopped and turned a saucy, smiling face up to him. "Why, thank you...I think. My second compliment today." She wrinkled her nose at him. "Refreshing. That is a compliment, isn't it?"

He hadn't meant to kiss her. But...that saucy face. The smile. Her lips parted invitingly, drawing him like a magnet. The touch was like a shot of brandy, potent and strong, spiraling through him, fusing them together. He knew she felt it, too, for her lips clung and she pressed closer, winding her arms around him.

"Lisa," he whispered, trying to understand this entirely new sensation...lust, powerful and urgent, but combined with a tender passionate yearning, a caring. "Oh, Lisa, I—"

She moved away, breaking the spell. "Thank you again for a fabulous evening. And I think we'd better say good-night." She spoke with finality. "See you in the morning," she said, closing the door behind him.

He stood for a moment, looking at the closed door. Then he walked slowly to his own room, trying to bring some order to his confused mind. He had never felt this way before. And never had he been so firmly refused.

Inside her room, Lisa leaned against her closed door, trying to get her emotions in order.

This feeling, sensuous and arousing. For a man who'd make an impossible husband.

Sex. That's what it was. She had several manuals on the subject, but hadn't delved into them yet. She was waiting until she found the right man.

One thing she did know. Sex could get you involved with the wrong man.

CHAPTER SIX

IN HIS own room, Scot tore off his coat and snatched at his tie, scarcely conscious of where he flung them. He was hot, frustrated...puzzled. One minute, a closeness like something out of this world. He had felt her response, warm, intimate passionate...urging, begging.... Then, wham! Like a douse of cold water! Coming on with that thanks...wonderful evening...good-night. Cool. Like she'd been untouched...bored, even.

He strode to the bar and poured himself a whiskey.

That, Ms. Wilson, is what is called a tease. It makes a guy pretty damn mad to be led on and then... He drank slowly, considering.

Okay, damn it. She didn't lead him on. She was just there...being herself, warm, open, friendly. And looking so darned appealing that he couldn't help but reach for her. He hadn't been prepared for the jolt. The touch of her lips had set him off like...well, there's no telling what might have happened had she not broken things off.

He set down his glass and slowly unbuttoned his shirt.

Thanks, Lisa, you've done us both a favor. Jeez, this kind of employer/employee liaison could really louse up a good business relationship. Which was exactly the reason he had not hired a type like Reba Morris.

He grinned. Maybe he should have hired Reba. He sure never felt any desire to touch her.

While Lisa... Well, he sure as hell meant to take care from now on. Didn't want to lose an excellent A.A. on account of a little flare of sexual persuasion!

Lisa, meanwhile, still leaned against her door, trying to catch her breath.

So this was what it was all about! This feeling...so explored in romance books, sex manuals, displayed on TV and movie screens. But reading about it was not like experiencing it yourself.

She hadn't known it could be so...so mixed up. She closed her eyes, remembering the rush of joy, so warm, so intimate, that she wanted to hold on to forever. A joy entwined with a raging fire that swept through her veins and brought her alive with an erotic yearning, so deep, so powerful that it took all of her resolve to deny her natural instincts. She backed away. Scared.

Sex. That's what it was. And why hadn't she experienced it before?

Because it takes two to tango! A man and a woman. Men, except for the Wells boys who had been like brothers, had been exempt from her life. At least, never personally involved with her.

So of course she would be bowled over by the first man who *really* kissed her. And of all people...her boss!

How had it come about? One minute he was Mr. Harding, the next he was Scot. One minute it was all business between them, the next a kind of easy banter and comfortable camaraderie at a conference. Intense business discussions...just that. But now...dancing. The boss/A.A. barriers between them were slipping!

She must not let this happen. They had established a good working relationship, and she didn't want to spoil it.

And yet... Her body still tingled from that kiss. The heat of passion still engulfed her, and she was almost overwhelmed by that erotic yearning so new to her. A longing so intense that...

Stop it! She covered her face with her hands, willing it to go away. She didn't want to feel this way about Scot Harding. Business aside, he was the exact opposite of the type of man she desired.

All right. She could manage. She had backed off tonight, hadn't she? She'd make darn sure they didn't get that close again.

She frowned, hoping the incident wouldn't spoil the good rapport that had been established between them. She didn't think it would. He was certainly more experienced and would not be as affected as she. If he thought of it at all, he would probably attribute the kiss to too much wine or the proper cap to an evening of fun.

So it had been, and she would forget about it, too, she decided, moving away from the door. In a way she was glad it had happened. A frigid woman, it was said, could spoil a marriage. She chuckled. It was just a kiss, but if it was a pre-amble to sex, she didn't think she was at all frigid.

Another thing...he had wanted to kiss her. Not only that. He had taken her dancing. Well, maybe that didn't count. He had felt guilty about spoiling her date with Sam. With Sam it would have been a date. Sam had taken her to lunch and really wanted her to go dancing with him. Just like men were always asking Reba Morris to go to lunch or somewhere!

Was it possible?

She walked across the room and critically surveyed herself in the full-length mirror. Shook her head. Sighed. Not a trace of that mysterious sensuality possessed by Reba.

But...not bad. The dress was certainly flattering. The gold color accentuated the frosting in her smart new haircut. The short skirt did show off her legs, her best feature, or so Loraine had said. And the new makeup did do something for her eyes.

She really didn't look too bad. In fact, pretty good. Why hadn't she noticed before?

Probably because she had been too busy measuring up as A.A. to the demanding Scot Harding. But she was too practical not to get her money's worth. So, despite her busy schedule, she had routinely followed all the treatments and advice offered by Hera's.

It had paid off! Her heart pounded with excitement. Now that she thought about it, there had been a few advances from other men, but she had been too involved with business to take them into account.

But now... Two dates in one day! And Sam Elliot, a connoisseur if there ever was one, had said she was beautiful. And even Scot had called her refreshing. The way he said it...he must have meant it as a compliment.

Two men. Never mind that they were both corporate-ladder-climbing types. If they were interested, there might be others who would also admire her.

Again she scrutinized herself carefully, turning this way and that. Not a bad package.

Maybe... No. *Really*. The miracle had happened. The preparation was over.

She was ready to begin her search. For the right man.

A spasm of curiosity gripped her. The right man. What would he be like?

The old jumping rope line spun through her mind. *Rich man, poor man, beggar man, thief! Doctor, lawyer, Indian chief!*

No! Her husband would not be chosen by a skipped rope. And not by a skip of the heart, either! Or any of those hit or miss chances that spelled doom for most marriages.

She had planned. She might not know exactly what he would be like. But she knew what he wouldn't be. He wouldn't be poor. Not rich maybe... but rich enough. And he wouldn't be a doctor, lawyer, or a chief of anything that would keep him away from the home fires. He would know how to laugh, how to play. He would like children, and he would love her. He would kiss her and...

She would not think about that!

But he would love her, wouldn't he? She had planned, prepared for that, too, hadn't she? She had the right qualifications, didn't she? And the right looks?

Again she studied herself in the mirror, more critically this time. She really was... well, almost beautiful. And what I'm lacking in looks, I'll make up in love and loyalty, and fun and tender loving care. I'll make you so happy, she promised that wonderful man who waited somewhere in her future.

Excitement raced through her. He was out there somewhere. She would find him. The hunt was on. She was on the brink of fulfilling all her plans, her hopes, her dreams.

This calls for a celebration, she thought. She went across the room to search through the minibar for wine.

Back at the mirror, she looked beyond herself, a sparkle of anticipation in her eyes. She held a glass of chardonnay in her left hand, pointed with her right, chortling, "Come out, come out, wherever you are! I'm on my way!"

It was their habit, when attending a conference, to meet at breakfast to plan the day's schedule. Lisa went down the next morning to meet him, feeling a little wary. An impossible working relationship if he felt . . . well, like she had felt for one crazy instant last night.

He rose, a sheaf of papers in his hand, as she approached their table. "Hi. Glad you came down early. I . . . I'm thinking of changing the schedule a bit."

"Oh?"

"Yes." Scot was glad for the moment of distraction while the waitress served her usual fruit and coffee. He had changed the schedule the minute Lisa walked toward him, each delicate curve enticingly revealed by the green knit jumpsuit that hugged her slender figure. Her gold-tinted hair and bright morning face... She took his breath away!

What the hell was wrong with him? His life was full of women, some more attractive than Lisa. Women are now a big part of the commercial world, and he treated them with the same commercial companionship as men, avoiding like the plague any personal intimacy. Socially? Well, okay, he was no celibate. But he was honest. His ban on marriage was always clearly understood, and he had never allowed any affair to become long-term and messy. He didn't want anyone hurt, and he had never been so affected that he couldn't back off.

But... what the hell was it about Lisa?

He swallowed, remembering last night. Watching her walk toward him.

He needed space. Time to get back on track.

"I thought, since I'm out here I ought to check by the L.A. office," he said now. "However, Stan should have these figures on the new legislation immediately. And he will need your input. So I thought you'd leave as planned this afternoon and I'll go on to L.A. Okay?"

"Sounds good to me." She was right about him, Lisa thought. Business as usual. Just as if last night had never happened. She was relieved. "Let's see... That comprehensive package you mentioned. What instructions about that, boss?"

*   *   *

Back in Wilmington, as soon as she could spare the time, Lisa delivered her presents from California. Mary Wells was delighted with the book on medicinal Chinese herbs, and Lisa helped plant the seeds in starter pots before she went on to see George's children. She found them on their living room floor among a litter of toys while Clarice reclined on the sofa, reading a paperback and munching chocolates.

"Only recreation I have," Clarice said, laying the book aside and getting up. "Let me get you a cold drink."

"Just water." Lisa said, following Clarice into the kitchen after diverting Betsy with the Chinese puzzle and Todd with the toy boat. "I'm watching my figure."

"Yeah, and I bet you're not the only one watching it." Clarice glanced enviously at Lisa. "How do you do it?"

Lisa, cool, comfortable, and chic, even in yellow shorts and top, laughed. "It ain't easy. But I've been on this really good diet. There's this great soup, nutritious and nonfattening. Want the recipe?" she asked, automatically clearing off the table as she spoke.

Clarice handed her a glass of water and looked a little sheepish as she took the dirty dishes from her. "Just doesn't seem worthwhile to clean up when everything's a mess the next minute."

"I know. Here, let me help you get these things out of the way." Lisa walked over to the sink and began to stack the dishwasher. In a few minutes, they had the kitchen fairly neat, and Lisa sat at the table to write out the recipe.

"Sounds yucky," Clarice said.

"It is not yucky. It's delicious. I served it to Mr. Harding and he didn't even know it was diet stuff, had a second helping."

"Your boss?" Clarice's eyes widened and she lost all interest in soup. "Lisa, he's gorgeous! I've been dying to ask. Do you...I mean, does he..."

"No, I don't! And he doesn't, either. The day you saw him was the one and only time he has been to my apartment and got saddled with your brats. He was there strictly on business. And that's all there is between us. Business!" Lisa said in one breath. She blocked out the thought of San Francisco. It had been strictly business since, hadn't it?

"Oh." Clarice looked disappointed. "But maybe... Hey, he's not married, is he?" And, when Lisa shook her head, "Well, then. Is he living with someone or got a steady or—?"

"I have no idea!" Lisa snapped, and didn't know why she was annoyed. It was Ms. Rodgers, his secretary, who complained, "I don't know why Scot's women don't restrict their chasing to after office hours. Gets pretty tiresome being the buffer...especially that Gwen woman who gives me that *he'll talk to me, just tell him it's Gwen* business." Lisa wondered if Gwen was the blonde who stopped by the office a couple of times to, as she put it, "Drag him off to lunch." Canceling out, Lisa remembered now, one of her scheduled business lunches with Scot. Not that she had minded. Why should she care whom he lunched with? Slept with, or lived with for that matter. "I know absolutely nothing about Mr. Harding's personal life. Nor do I care about it," she said. "Here's the recipe."

"Thanks," Clarice said, rather absently. "Well, if he's not married and hasn't got anybody... Heck, Lisa, if I were you—"

"Oh, Clarice, you should take the kids to see that new movie, *The Demon and Davey Dawson*," Lisa cut in. "It's so funny." She kept talking about it, not giving Clarice a chance to say another word about Scot Harding. She didn't want to hear it.

Driving home, Lisa realized she had spent very little time with the kids, whom she had really come to see. Just to play a few games with Betsy or to hug sweet, cuddly Todd. Still, she was glad she had spent the time with Clarice, who seemed to need the diversion. She had even dropped the computer course. If she would bestir herself, like Mary. But Clarice wasn't interested in things that interested Mary... gardening, decorating. And much as she loved the children, too much baby talk could become boring. And George's time schedule, combined with his fad for sports...

Lisa sighed. That's what came of marrying too young, with stars in your eyes, and no planning or preparation for what you really wanted.

When she arrived home, Lisa found a card from Ruth, currently cruising in the Greek Isles. Wondering if she really was "having a delightful time," Lisa thought of Reba Martin, Ruth's composite if there ever was one. Reba evidently knew what she wanted and worked hard for it. Busy clawing to get to the top executive office, or trying to seduce some man as competitive as she. Lisa doubted that either would bring ultimate happiness. Be careful what you want, you might get it.

The thought startled her. Was she slipping into the Ruth/Reba game?

No! Indeed she wasn't.

Are you sure?

Okay, I like the money. And I mean to do a good job for which I'm paid. But I certainly have no ambition to go further.

Stuck where you are, huh?

No. Lisa threw down the card and continued the argument with herself. Well, not exactly. Heck! Getting...finding what you want ain't easy. She had acquired the attributes, prettied the package, and...

Takes two to tango. And the men she met through her corporate position were, of course, corporate types. Wrong. Even the travel had not afforded the exposure she hoped. Too busy with business. Not that she had done too much traveling lately. Scot seemed to prefer going alone.

After thinking the matter over, she had increased her time on the golf course, finally joining a country club. Not too exclusive for her touch, but exclusive enough to attract a fairly wealthy bachelor with time on his hands and a penchant for golf. So far she hadn't encountered one.

Late Friday afternoon, she was with Harding when Hal Stanford barged into his office.

"Chief, I've got to cancel out on tomorrow's golf. Little League. You see, I'm the Golden Bear's coach and—"

"Little League!" Harding's face was livid. "Look, Stan, this was set up a week ago, before I left for the Bahamas, and you agreed—"

"I know. But this is the playoff, an all-day thing. It was scheduled for last Saturday, but we got rained out."

"Stan, it's not the World Series!"

Stan grinned. "It is to my son."

Scot wasn't grinning. "This isn't just a golf game. I went to a lot of trouble. Allen Dobbs, the senator who is sponsoring this bill that's likely to cramp our style and set a precedent for other states, just happens to be in town this weekend and happens to be a friend of my friend, Jake Mason, who has arranged this friendly golf game so I can casually drop a bug in the senator's ear apprising him of the damage such a bill could do to our clients as well as to our firm. And you want to cancel out." Scot paused for breath, exasperated.

"Heck, Scot, there must be a dozen guys who could fill in for me."

"Not one of which has any savvy about what we need to casually discuss!"

"I do," Lisa said.

Both men, who had forgotten that she was there, stared at her.

"You do what?" Harding finally asked.

"Know what needs to be casually discussed."

Scot looked exasperated. "That point I will concede," he said. "But this, dear lady, is not a business conference and must not appear to be so. This requires more than a knowledge of insurance. We need someone who can play golf."

"I can."

Stan looked skeptical and Scot smiled but shook his head. "I mean, who can really play."

"How about a ten handicap?" She returned their unbelieving stares with one of smug satisfaction. She could prove it. And she could fill the bill of that foursome. Further, Scot Harding's club was far more prestigious than hers. Teaming with wealth. And there must surely be a few bachelors among the members.

CHAPTER SEVEN

FROM the passenger seat of Scot's Porsche, Lisa surveyed the grounds of the Overland Country Club. Tall, stately trees and spacious lawns, having the stamp of old money and gracious living, artfully concealing such amenities as tennis courts, Olympic swimming pool, eighteen-hole golf course and practice tees.

"Such a beautiful setting," she said.

Scot, who had viewed the setting all his life and inherited the family life membership, merely grunted. He was apprehensive. Jake had a six handicap and he suspected the senator was on the same level. Neither would appreciate being teamed with a rank beginner. Not that he doubted Lisa's word. But...well, some people were apt to stretch a thing like a handicap.

"They're here already. There's Jake," he said, nodding toward the pro shop as he pulled into a parking slot. Jake, a sandy-haired young man almost as tall as Scot, came over to help retrieve their bags from the trunk. "Hi," he said. "I've already signed us in. We have a half hour or so to loosen up." He smiled at Lisa, but shot an inquisitive glance toward Scot.

"Lisa Wilson," Scot said. "She's filling in for Stan."

"Good. Glad to have you. I'm Jake, Jake Mason."

They walked toward the pro shop and were introduced to the senator, a short stocky man who appeared to be in his mid-forties. "None of that 'your honor' stuff," he admonished jovially. "I'm here to play. And my name is Al!"

Scot noticed that both the senator and Jake were casting admiring eyes toward Lisa. Yep, those shorts gave an excellent view of those perfect legs. The green sleeveless shirt and shorts sent a bright greenish cast to her blue eyes. And with that golf cap perched jauntily on her head... He took a deep breath, glad he had trained himself to be immune. Okay, right outfit. But could she really play golf?

He was aware that that question was also in the minds of the other two men as they settled in separate stalls at the practice tee. Each bent to his own clubs and bucket of balls, but all eyes were on Lisa. She paused for a moment, taking a look as if to accustom herself to the range. Then she set a ball on the tee, took out her short iron and stepped into position, legs apart, eyes on the ball. Swung. She seemed unaware of the awed gasps as the ball sailed high and straight almost reaching the one hundred yard marker. Not one, but three or four as she changed to a longer iron.

Scot breathed a sigh of relief, but only Jake spoke. "Great iron play, Lisa."

"Thanks," she said, bending to select another ball.

She continued to display the same skill as she advanced from irons to woods. The men, while practicing their own shots, continued to watch her. When they took their places to tee off, it was Jake who suggested that he and Lisa should team up against the other two. "Makes a pretty even match, don't you think?"

"Sure," Scot agreed, conceding that it did, and wondering why it irked him to ride with the senator in one cart while Jake, with Lisa close beside him, followed in another. Hadn't he been trying to distance himself from Lisa except at the office? He had been pretty burned up when he had to substitute her for Stan. Anyway, wasn't this the opportunity he wanted? To talk business and politics with the senator?

The senator was agreeable to such discussion, and they did talk openly and compatibly. But Scot's attention often wavered, focusing on the other pair. Mighty damn cozy. So what else was new? Wasn't that Jake's mode of operation? The prettier the woman, the cozier!

Hell! Why should Lisa's exposure to a playboy like Jake concern him? He concentrated on the conversation with Senator Dobbs, but his gaze constantly strayed toward Lisa.

Lisa was enjoying herself. As soon as she had a glimpse of the other women golfers at the club, she knew she had been right to splurge on her own deceptively simple outfit. She looked right. And the hours of practice hadn't failed her. She could hold her own. And the charming young man beside her made a most agreeable companion.

"Why haven't I seen you before?" he asked. "Where have you been, pretty lady?"

"Busy earning a living," she said, enjoying but determined not to succumb to his flirtatious advances. She wasn't so crass as to ask his business, but "birds of a feather." A friend of Scot's... probably the same type.

"Have you known Scot long?" she asked.

"All my life. Prep school roommates, same frat, same clubs... business, too."

"Oh." She was right.

Not quite right, she discovered sometime later, when she stood with the senator, watching Jake walk toward the sand trap where his ball had landed. Scot, whose ball had landed near the trap, was with him.

"Scot tells me you're his assistant," the senator said.

She nodded.

"So you're part of the insurance gang, too!"

"And you're the man who's going to take us on," she teased.

"Somebody has to."

"Well, don't be too hard on us," she said, smiling. "You know how much we are needed. Hey, look at that!" she exclaimed as Jake's ball spiraled out of the trap and onto the green three feet from the cup. "He's really good!"

"Ought to be," the senator said. "Spends most of his time on one golf course or another. Beats the hell out of me every time he comes to Dover."

"He's a good friend? I mean... have you known him long?"

"About eight years. Married a cousin of his. He was in the wedding."

"I see."

"And yes, he is a good friend. Especially to the party."

"Oh."

"Very generous with donations. 'Course it hardly makes a drop in the Mason millions. Good shot, Jake," he called as the other two strode toward them. "We need a birdie, Scot. These two are well ahead."

Lisa was quiet. Everything fell into place. The Mason millions. Mason. The Mason Building. Mason Shopping Center. A large part of the vast Mason real estate holdings were insured by Safetech. She had even heard of Jacob Wellington Mason, the Third. But somehow she had never connected him with Scot's casual references to a Jake he had to meet, or call, or check with about something.

She did connect him now. Jacob Wellington Mason. Young, handsome, rich. With time on his hands. Not exactly retired, but as good as.

She suddenly felt shy as she climbed onto the cart for the next trek. Preparing and planning to capture a nebulous somebody who would make a perfect husband was one thing. But Jake was a real person. Lisa's whole nature balked at the very idea of trying to manipulate a real person into anything.

Oh, heck! What was she thinking about anyway? She hadn't the least notion how to entice a man. All she knew how to do was ... well, just be herself. It was a beautiful day. She would just have fun.

She did not forget her purpose for being there. She was especially charming to Senator Dobbs and tried to serve as a backup for Scot.

Scot did not fail to notice. She's better than Stan would have been, he finally admitted. Stan would have zeroed in with hard, cold facts, which might have irritated the senator. Lisa's definitely feminine approach was conciliatory and probably more effective. "Oh, you are absolutely right, sir. Regulations are necessary." Then she would flash an impish grin. "But, please, not a noose around our neck. Protection is our business. We need space and resources to deliver full benefits."

He had been right to bring her. Why had he hesitated?

You know damn well why! You can hardly keep your distance during business hours.

But I'm managing. As long as I concentrate strictly on business and keep my eyes averted from her.

Like they are now, huh?

But he couldn't help watching her. He grinned as she readied herself to tee off. Typical golfer's pose. A pause as she prepared for the shot. Then her arms swung back and quickly forward, and...wham! The impact of the club sent the ball straight down the course. So much power in that tiny figure. "Good shot, Lisa!"

"Thanks, Scot," she said, her face glowing. Appealing. Refreshing.

"Yeah, you guys are two up with one hole to go. We can't win," he said, his eyes riveted on her as she left the tee and strode down the fairway toward the last hole.

"A good day's work," he told her when he drove her home. "Didn't know you could hit the ball like a pro. More important, you really impressed the senator."

"Nuts. You made all the points."

"But you made him listen. You have a way of doing that. I owe you one."

"No. Just part of the job, sir."

"Well, you deserve a bonus. Sorry I have an appointment tonight," he lied. After watching her all day... if he took her out to dinner tonight, he sure as hell couldn't keep his hands off her. As long as he avoided any too personal contact...

Lisa might have dismissed Jake Mason from her mind, but he had not dismissed her. There was something about her. Different.

It couldn't be said that Jake Mason was a womanizer. It was just that women had a habit of falling at his feet. He took their adulation for granted, just as he did his great wealth. His habit was to enjoy whichever woman interested him at the moment, casually, just as he dabbled occasionally at whichever part of the family business perked his momentary interest.

Lisa Wilson sparked his interest. Possibly because she made no effort to spark it. No flirtatious attempts, neither coy nor boldly seductive, to gain his attention. No come-on invitations, neither suggestively personal nor carefully impersonal. "I'm having a few people over and why don't you join us?" No flattery. Nothing. At least nothing that he was accustomed to receiving.

Yes, Lisa Wilson was different. Frank, open, friendly. Just having a hell of a lot of fun in a friendly game of golf. Almost like one of the guys, except there was no mistaking the femininity. She was not a beauty, at least not his usual type. But there was a kind of freshly scrubbed prettiness about her. Cute as a button in those golf togs.

"Yes, I enjoyed it, too," Lisa said, surprised by his call.

"So why don't we try it again? Just the two of us. A little friendly competition."

"Competition? You and me?" Lisa spoke with her usual frankness. "That's no competition. That's murder! You hit the ball a ton."

He laughed. "Oh, I wouldn't say that. You're pretty good."

"And you're perfect."

"Okay. Why don't we call it a practice session?"

"Oh, would you?" she said, genuinely pleased. "That would be great."

"Sure. How does Saturday sound?"

"Just fine. Only..." She hesitated. Great for her, but he was almost a professional, way above her standard. "Are you sure it wouldn't be a bother?"

"No bother at all. A pleasure. Shall I pick you up at...shall we say eight?"

That was the beginning. There were two other golf games. He took her to dinner, and they went dancing afterward. He took her for a sail on his schooner. He had season tickets to all the shows, and had invited her to join him for a play this Saturday night. It was a play she particularly wanted to see and she looked forward to it. In fact, she was enjoying herself immensely. She liked Jake, and she had never before received this kind of attention from any man.

Saturday night as they were leaving the theater, he suggested that they should "Run over to Bermuda for a week or so. We could leave tomorrow."

She stared at him, realizing for the first time where all the fun was leading. A week together in Bermuda wouldn't be just dinner, dancing, and a casual good-night kiss. It would mean an intimacy she was not ready for.

Not like the time in San Francisco when she was able to limit Scot to a kiss. A kiss that had sent her senses reeling.

Scot. Did he kiss that Gwen woman like that? Did her body go limp with a delightful erotic yearning? Did they—?

"Hey!" Jake playfully snapped his fingers before her. "Come back. Where did you go?"

"Oh. I...I was thinking."

"So what do you think? Can you be ready to leave tomorrow?"

Play it cool, she cautioned, trying to get a grip on herself. Why was she thinking about Scot? "Leave tomorrow? For a week or so?" She managed a chuckle. "Idiot. You forget I'm a working girl."

"There are such things as vacations."

"Oh, sure. But not the see-you-in-a-week-or-so, boss. I'm-off-tomorrow-for-Bermuda kind." What would Scot think? Darn it! Why couldn't she get him out of her mind?

Jake laughed. "Okay. Set your own schedule. When would you like to go?"

Now she wondered what Jake was thinking. That she was the kind of woman who would go blithely off to spend a week with a guy... For what? Fun and games, laced with sex? No commitment or honorable intentions, or...

Okay, so she was a prude. But... well, what did Jake have in mind? She evaded the question, as well as the implication. No matter what Jake Mason had in mind, she had her own agenda. It didn't include jaunting off at the drop of a hat to spend an intimate weekend with him or any other guy.

"Let me know," he said when he left. "I'm free anytime."

She shut her door, pondering. Free anytime. True. As far as she could discern, Jake was unencumbered by business or anything else. Time. Money. All the potential for an excellent participating marriage partner.

She was on the hunt, wasn't she? Again she thought of that night in San Francisco. She had stood in front of that mirror, admiring herself, and promising a wonderful unknown somebody that she was coming for him. Oh, she had been so cocky that night. Because of . . . Scot. It wasn't just the kiss, the crazy jumble of emotions it evoked in her. It was that he, too, was shaken by that powerful surge of passion. She had felt his body tense, then press against hers . . . demanding, begging. His touch had been tender, but undeniably possessive. His eyes had held a hungry adoration that made her feel . . . like a woman. A beautiful, appealing, exciting woman.

She had pushed him away, her body still tingling with wanting, but the excitement remained. Like a gift . . . the knowledge that he desired her. That she was a desirable woman.

It had gone to her head. Given her such confidence. Savoring a glass of wine, she had stood before that mirror, making all kinds of extravagant promises.

Now she sighed. The excitement had faded.

No. Not exactly. For her plans had been in progress long before. That night had given her confidence that she was ready to begin her search.

And she had begun, hadn't she? She had joined that golf club, and . . .

And nothing. Jake Mason had just fallen into her lap, so to speak. When she wasn't even looking. And, to tell the truth, she had just been having fun with him, like with one of the Wells boys.

But...think about it. She couldn't find a better match if she searched forever.

She sat on her bed, slipped off her shoes. No reason to be ashamed of what she was thinking. Just going out with a guy, enjoying his company, wasn't manipulating.

Evidently he also enjoyed her company. He kept calling, taking her out. That was the way it happened. You met someone. He liked you. You liked him. If he would make a perfect husband...

Marriage might not be what Jake had in mind.

She would wait and see.

"Good morning, boss. Here's your coffee."

"Thanks. Just what I've been waiting for." Scot smiled. It wasn't the coffee. It was the fact that she brought it, same as always. The sight of that gold-tinted hair, the bright face, the cheerful voice evoked the lift, set the tone for the day. "Let's see. We've got the Spaulding thing today, haven't we?"

"Right. I brought the file. Thought we'd better review it before we meet him at lunch." She sat beside his desk and opened a folder.

That's what he liked. Her efficiency. The way she anticipated every need. Made things easy. Best A.A. he ever had, he thought as they delved into the day's agenda.

Strictly business, and he meant to keep it that way. If the sight of her gave him a lift, if he felt possessively proud of her support at a conference or business luncheon... well, so be it. There was as far as it went. No hanky-panky at the office. No traveling together.

Only... well, it would really be unfair not to take her to the East African conference in Nairobi. The main issue on the agenda was the Ugandan expansion which she had almost single-handedly programmed.

He grinned. Arranged everything with her usual efficiency in the middle of her bed in a messy bedroom with two active brats on her hand!

"You know, I think Mr. Spaulding is concerned about..." Lisa stopped, staring at him. "What's so funny, boss?"

"Oh. Nothing." He cleared his throat. "You know, Lisa... this East African conference. I think you should be a part of it."

CHAPTER EIGHT

LISA was excited about the trip to Africa. She looked forward to seeing the wild animals roaming freely in their natural habitat, mile upon mile of beautiful terrain. She planned, with Scot's permission, to indulge in a mini holiday. She would stay on for three days after the conference to go on safari in one of the parks, she wasn't sure which. On the plane, she pored over travel brochures, trying to decide.

"Which do you think?" she asked Scot who was seated beside her.

He shrugged. "Toss a coin."

"Oh, that's stupid! I have to choose. When will I be this way again? And see, here..." She rambled on, excitedly exclaiming over the various sights. "So little time and so much to see. I just don't know which."

"Well, don't ask me. Safaris are not my thing," he said, and returned to his newspaper.

Lisa's lips tightened. He hadn't even glanced at the colorful brochures. In fact, he had hardly glanced at her during the entire trip. He stayed buried in newspapers and magazines, or studied conference data which they had already thoroughly explored before they left. He acted like she wasn't there. Or like he wished she wasn't.

She grinned. Maybe he wished it was Gwen, the beautiful, seated beside him instead.

It hit her. He had not asked her to accompany him on a single conference since San Francisco. Until this one. And now he was keeping his distance. Like she had the pox or something!

Or... San Francisco. Good grief! Did he think she was after him or...

Why, you arrogant so and so! I'd like to remind you that it was *I* who pushed *you* out of my bedroom, Mr. Conceited Scot Harding. Okay, so I might have given the impression that... She blushed, remembering how she had been thrown off base for a minute or two. Don't let a slight glandular reaction go to your head, buddy! I wouldn't have a corporate-ladder-climbing executive like you if you were the last man on earth! So there!

Oh, good heavens! Maybe she was the conceited one. Sensitive? Because Scot Harding has more on his mind than you?

Ridiculous. She put the brochures away, and gazed out the window, trying to see the ocean far below.

Scot glanced at her out of the corner of his eye. She could get so enthusiastic about *anything*. And when she did... her eyes would light up, that dimple in the corner of her mouth would dance, and he could hardly keep his eyes off her. Which he had vowed he would do. Of course he could travel with Lisa and keep his mind on business.

From the bustling Nairobi airport, they were whisked by limousine to Nairobi's Safari Hotel. Fatigued by jet lag, Lisa went directly to her room and to sleep. She had to be ready for the first conference session, scheduled early the next morning.

Lisa felt apprehensive that morning as she entered the room for Scot's kick-off speech. There was sure to be the usual competition and vying for position that accompanied any large expansion plan. Projects to be discussed at this conference were not only extensive, but complicated, since they involved all the major East African countries. Compromises and conciliations would be necessary, and not easy to accomplish, even for the master negotiator she knew Scot Harding to be.

If he shared her apprehensions, there was no sign of it as he faced the delegates to open the conference. Cool and correct in a lightweight well-cut tan suit, matching silk shirt and complimentary tie, he exuded an air of assurance that they were here to do business and he was the man with whom to do it. He was in charge. His relaxed stance, genial air, and affable smile set everyone at ease. Within two minutes of his opening statements, they were with him, anticipating a venture in which they would all participate, all succeed. Charisma. Her unruly heart gave a lurch. Pride in his mode of operation, she reasoned, ignoring a strange sensation she refused to identify. She listened with avid attention until his closing statement. "Our responsibilities are to see that the strategic pieces of the Safetech expansion in East Africa are addressed, resolved, and within the projected yield."

How many times, in how many places had she heard him express this same sentiment? *Our responsibility... to build the world's economy.* To expand business that kept people working, fed and clothed millions.

Again, and not for the first time, Lisa felt that little jolt of pride. She liked the way Scot worked, drawing people with him, accomplishing what was needed. Her sentiments were echoed by Mr. Mamboso, the Ugandan Minister of Finance, who was seated beside her at dinner that night. "I like your Mr. Harding," he said.

"My...?" Lisa stopped, the hot blush receding. He meant the company's Mr. Harding, not hers.

Mamboso seemed not to notice her hesitation. "He is direct, never dodging any issue. He clearly outlined the plan, the problems, and the way we should proceed. I wish I could hire him as Director of Tourism.''

''Oh?''

''We could use him. Tourism,'' he said, ''is our biggest industry as well as one of our biggest problems. We are dedicated to preserving our wildlife of course. But animals need space as well as people. Providing for both is difficult.''

''Yes, I can see that. But you seem to be doing an excellent job of handling it.'' Lisa looked up at him, her smile bright. He could advise her. Eagerly she launched into a discussion of the various safaris.

Scot did not join the short tour which had been scheduled for those interested on the morning of the last day. He spent the morning with the ministers of finance. It was productive. Corporate taxes demanded of foreign investors were fair, but one had to be sure they were equitable.

His thoughts were now on the projects awaiting his attention at the home office. He reviewed them as he packed, and his mind focused on possible resolutions as he went down to eat. He was leaving the next day, and should be back in the office on Tuesday. Would that be in time to—?

''Oh, Scot, you should have come with us.'' Lisa, a Polaroid camera slung over her shoulder, was evidently just returning from the tour. ''They drove us around the park and I got such good pictures." She looked like an excited child, he thought, in those yellow shorts, her hair tousled, her eyes bright. "Now I'm good and hungry. If it's okay, I'll join you and show you my pictures."

Scot nodded. "Good."

"See!" she said, spreading the pictures before him when they were seated. "That's a lioness with her cubs. Aren't they adorable?"

"Yes," he said, but he was looking at her. Thinking. He had traveled all over the world and never bothered with a camera.

"I almost missed the antelope. He came so close, but they are so swift. I did miss the leopard. There was so much to see and our time was so short that . . ." She paused while the waiter took their orders. Then she turned to him. "I've decided where to go. I was talking to Mr. Mamboso last night."

"Yes. So I noticed." He had been at another table next to the Tanzanian executive, trying to listen to several complaints. But his eyes had strayed toward Lisa, head tilted, totally absorbed, as if nothing interested her but what Mamboso was saying. What had he been saying? "An interesting man, huh?"

"Oh, yes! He told me so much about this country."

"I see." Yes, she had that knack of drawing people out.

"He says the land itself is so beautiful. Lake Nakuru where the flamingos come to feed, covering it like a mammoth pink blanket. And Victoria Falls, the largest in the entire world. Oh, there's so much I'd like to see!"

Scot wondered if Mamboso got the same lift as he. Just from her voice, her enthusiasm.

"And I haven't begun to see all the animals. There are rhinoceroses, elephants, tigers, hyenas, baboons—"

"Boa constrictors, pythons, and puff adders," he added.

"Yes, but I doubt I will see those."

"Thank God." Darn, she's even enthusiastic about snakes.

But when lunch was served, Lisa picked at her salad, her enthusiasm dimming a bit. "Of course I won't see the falls."

"I don't see why not," he said.

"They're in Zambia. I've decided on the Nairobi Treetop safari. Shucks," she reflected. "I wouldn't have time or money for more."

"We could hire a plane," he said impulsively.

"We? A plane?" She stared at him.

"Cover a lot of territory in a short period of time." He cleared his throat. "Might be good business."

"Business?"

"We carry the insurance on most of the safari camps. Wouldn't hurt to do a little checking.

Since we're here," he added, wondering whatever had come over him.

"Yes, since we are here," she echoed, her mouth a round circle of surprise.

"Now, which areas interest you most?" he asked as he began to eat with surprising appetite, not looking at her.

"Well..." A private plane that would whisk them from one magic spot to another! She was a little awestruck. But she was not about to look a gift horse in the mouth.

Scot had Lisa change his departure time. Back in his room, he unpacked and made arrangements to hire a plane and a guide. On his own. Sure wouldn't be fair to charge it to the company since it was not scheduled.

Again he wondered what had come over him.

Lisa. She had looked so eager. And she had made this conference so easy. Not only the preparation, but she had been at the ready every minute with whatever information he needed. She had earned a day or two off to see more of the country about which she was so excited.

He ignored certain repressed emotions that threatened to surface...a longing to share her enthusiasm, a reluctance to take the long trip home without her beside him....

He called off the matters awaiting his attention at the home office. Things would keep for a few days. He placed a call to Wilmington, and spent a long time on the phone. Pertinent matters were delegated.

He told himself he was doing it for Lisa. Certainly not for himself. Tours were not his thing. Animals? He had lived in New York most of his life and, as a child, had been taken to the zoo many times. And there had been Rex, his golden retriever, so much a part of his boyhood. Horses on the family compound. But that was about as far as it went.

He had not expected the emotion that gripped him when he stood beside Lisa in an open-roofed van and lifted his binoculars to see an antelope dart across a plain that stretched as far as the eye could see. He was infused with a feeling of serenity and exaltation. Joy that they were there, a part of it all. He reached for her hand, glad they shared it together, entranced by the immensity, the sheer beauty of the land.

"It's so overwhelmingly beautiful," Lisa whispered. "Do you suppose the Leakeys are right? That this is really where civilization began?"

"Could be," he said, thinking of their short tour through the museum which contained artifacts, evidence, according to the Leakeys, of man's first appearance on earth. "Certainly contains all the early trappings."

"Yes. The Garden of Eden. Can't you see it? Man and beast living peaceably together. The lion lying with the lamb. The snake upright—"

His bellow of laughter interrupted her. "No, I can't see it. What would the lion eat? And what would the snake stand on?"

"Oh, you. No faith. And no imagination, either," she chided as they crossed a bridge to the Ark, the rather luxurious lodge where they would spend the night. It was perched high above a mammoth water hole and a salt lick, the largest in Kenya. Several animals would gather there each night, and they would be privileged to view them from the Ark's bunk.

They dined in the luxurious restaurant, and, tired from their long trek, retired to their separate rooms. Lisa tumbled immediately into bed, and was awakened by a loud buzz, the signal that animals had appeared at the watering hole. She threw a jacket over her pajamas and hastened down, not intending to miss anything.

Scot, still in his safari gear, was waiting for her. Evidently he had not bothered to retire. In a few minutes they took their turn in the bunk, the glassed-in cubicle where guests, a few at a time, were permitted to view the animals.

"We're in the cage," Lisa chuckled, pressing her face against the glass as if she could get a closer look. "And they're out there, roaming free, doing their own thing. Oh, you big bully!"

she cried as a big water hog pushed aside a smaller one in the watering hole.

Scot laughed, his eyes more on Lisa than the scene below. So intently interested, so vibrantly alive. She enhanced each moment.

"Do you suppose animals think?" she asked.

"Of course. That big elephant rolling on his back in that salt bed, is thinking, *Take that! Irritating itchy bugs!*"

"Silly. I know they think about eating and sleeping and getting rid of ticks, but..." She sighed. "I guess they just live, doing what comes naturally. They leave the problems to people like us...like you."

"Me?" he asked, puzzled, but drinking in the you're-so-wonderful look in her eyes.

"I mean, people like you who are in charge of the world's economy, keep us working, and...oh, you know." She seemed embarrassed and hastily added, "Mr. Mambosa was very impressed with you."

"He's okay, too." But he liked the way she was looking at him. He didn't want her to go back to her room. Away from him.

"Let's have a drink," he said, motioning toward the bar.

She looked down at herself. "I don't think I'm dressed for it," she said.

"You're beautiful," he said. "You'd be beautiful in anything."

"Why, thank you," she said with an impish grin. "That's very welcome talk to a girl who was bedeviled by buck teeth, knock knees, and three Wells boys."

"I don't believe it."

"Believe it. I was a horror." She stepped back, put her knees together, and made a face as she protruded her upper teeth over her lower lip.

He roared with laughter as he led her into the bar. "Yes, I see. Truly an ugly duckling," he said, pulling out her chair at a window booth.

She nodded as she took her seat. "I was. And Joey, Bob, and George Wells reminded me every day. That's why I have such a complex."

"Yes, I've noticed. Tell me, lady, how did you manage to transform into such a beautiful swan?"

"All that hard work at Hera's. And Aunt Ruth. She's magic."

"Tell me."

"About Aunt Ruth?"

"Everything. I want to know all about you."

It seemed a time for confiding. Sitting in her pajamas, in an almost-empty bar, sipping drinks, and looking out at a dark sky dotted with stars, she told him. About Aunt Ruth, temporarily in London, who had supplied braces and dancing lessons, the bullying of the Wells boys, and Mary Wells's tender loving care.

"A pretty full well-rounded life," he said. "No wonder you're so beautiful. It's from the inside."

It wasn't so much what he said, but the way he looked at her. Warm and loving, making her feel like she was special. A desirable woman whose appeal went far deeper than glands. She was engulfed by a hot ripple of pleasure, and felt suddenly shy.

"I'm doing this all wrong. I should be listening to you, according to this book."

"What book?"

"Never mind. Tell me about Scot Harding before Safetech."

"Rather mundane, I'm afraid. School, camps, basketball, golf."

She stared at him. "That sounds very institutional. Didn't you have a home?"

He gave a wry smile, took a sip of vodka. "Oh, sure. A big home. Lots of land, trees, horses, servants."

"But... surely you had a family."

"That, too. A brother and a father. Don't remember much about my mother. She died when I was five."

"Oh. I'm sorry." Of course she had lost her parents, too, when she was very young. But there had been Mary.

"Did you have a favorite aunt or... someone into whose lap you could climb when you got a bruise or got teased?"

He shook his head. "Nope. All male servants, and I'm a little short on relatives. But...oh, don't look like that. I had a heck of a good life. Not even any bullying. Chuck, my brother, is a couple of years older, but we got on well together. My father, too, when he was home. Lots of fun, actually...golf, tennis, the works."

"And you never missed..." She paused, not sure how to phrase all the tender loving care of a Mary. "A woman's touch?" she finally finished.

"Maybe Chuck does," he said with a smile. "At least he's married three times, looking for it."

"And struck out," she mused, almost to herself. "Is that why you're afraid to look? Why you've never... Oh, good grief! It's late." She stood up, appalled at herself. A big difference between listening and prying. "I'd better go if I want to make that wake-up call tomorrow," she said, and fled.

He stood and watched her leave. Hating to see her go.

Wondering. What was all this psychological stuff? Chuck was searching and he was afraid to.

Bull! He had all the woman's touch he wanted. And when it got to be too much, he could back off.

Even from Lisa. Actually, she was a double taboo. Not only a valuable business partner, she

was also a woman on the hunt for a husband.
And he was not in the market for marriage.

Hell, if he could back off from Lisa, he could
back off from anybody.

Beautiful, exciting, vivacious Lisa, whether hot
and dusty in a van under a burning sun, or
sharing intimate thoughts in a dimly lit bar...
She was a delightful companion. It was as if they
had reached a plateau, a kinship, almost spiritual.

Something else. He had not, this time, tried to
kiss her. Not once. No matter how many times
he had wanted to.

That said something, didn't it? No need to be
concerned about working closely with her, or
traveling together.

CHAPTER NINE

BACK in Wilmington, it was business as usual, at a faster and more gruesome pace. Scot was a tireless worker, and Lisa found herself scrambling to keep up. Moreover, she became anxious for him. He was so tense, so meticulous about each detail of each project to be reviewed, decision to be made, problem to be solved. Everything. As if the whole Safetech empire rested on his shoulders. Too much.

She was irritated when other officials dumped their problems on him, problems they were paid to handle. She tried to shield him as best she could. But sometimes things got out of hand. Especially with Reba. "I've got to get with Scot on this. Is he free for lunch?" Her insinuating just-between-the-two-of-us air made Lisa wonder. Were there after hours twosomes, as well? She tried to shrug aside that sharp prick of irritation. It was certainly no concern of hers.

Anyway, Scot's manner toward Reba was impersonal. Almost as if he was being careful to keep it that way, Lisa thought. Conciliatory, though. Always made the lunch if he was free. Well, why not! Reba was Personnel Officer, and in a company with an international work force, highly competitive, of course they had sensitive changes to discuss. Oh, good grief! I've got more to think about than whatever Reba Morris's discussing with... whomever.

Still, she was irked when Reba burst in upon them one afternoon. Lisa had remained with Scot after office hours to catch up on a mountain of paperwork.

"Oh, I'm sorry. I thought..." Reba gave Lisa a cursory glance before turning again to Harding. "I thought you were alone. I need to talk to you."

"Oh?"

Reba seemed to flinch under his questioning stare. Then she smiled. "It can wait until you've finished here. After... could I treat you to dinner? Something I need to thrash out with you... about the internees."

Lisa's fingers tightened on her pencil. They had just begun to make a little headway and Reba interrupted to talk about hiring a few students.

Scot voiced her irritation. "So, thrash away. What's wrong?"

"Nothing's wrong, not yet. But..." She glanced again toward Lisa. "It's rather touchy."

"Good Lord, Reba! What's so touchy about hiring a few students?"

This time he sounded so impatient that Reba became apologetic, albeit rather defiant. "Scot, I wouldn't bother you about this now, except that this Mr. Glover phoned me this afternoon and tomorrow he's bringing this boy you promised to hire.''

"Glover? Oh, yes, I remember. He's the boy's sponsor. He spoke to me at Rotary and I meant to alert you that he was bringing him in.''

"You knew he was a high school dropout and on parole from the youth authority?''

"Yes.''

"Scot, we already have more internees than we scheduled for,'' Reba said. "It's difficult to find places and work for the ones we already have.''

"Frankly, Reba, I don't expect much work from these kids. The program is for them. An opportunity to observe and learn.''

"And just what do you expect a parolee to learn?''

"That there are other ways to make a living than stealing hubcaps.''

"Oh, Scot, for goodness' sake, you don't mean we should hire him. I could explain that we're overloaded and—''

"Hire him. Glover says the boy has been shunted from one foster home to another and has gotten off track. But he says he's a bright kid with real potential. If given a push in the right direction... Oh, hire him, Reba! Surely we can handle one more.'' He got up and opened the door for her. "Please, excuse us. I'm really rather busy.''

Not too busy to fight for a kid who needs a push, Lisa thought. She remembered his words when he'd instituted the program. "Our young people are the future, both for us and the country. They need a chance to see what's going on." He had said he was being practical. She smiled. She would call it compassion. For one lost boy.

Yes, Scot Harding was quite a man. A man who needs some tender loving care, Lisa thought as he walked to the window and stretched. He pushed himself too hard. Just back from a hurried trip to Denver yesterday, a meeting last night, he'd skipped lunch...

"We need a break," she said. "Let's take this to my place. I'll fix a snack and we can finish up."

"Good idea," he said. "Only we could go out or have something sent in. You shouldn't trouble."

"No trouble." A restaurant would be crowded and noisy. If they stayed here, he'd just keep working. At her place, while she fixed something he could take a much needed breather.

Her apartment was not the mess it had been the last time he had seen it. It was clean and neat, and rather homey, Scot thought, glancing at the scattered magazines and the vase of long-stemmed roses on the coffee table. Did she buy those herself or did someone send them? he wondered.

"I won't be long," Lisa said. "Why don't you stretch out on the couch and rest while you wait?"

Scot was too tired to resist the suggestion. He took off his shoes and stretched out, and, almost immediately dozed off.

A good time to test the book, Lisa thought, laughing at herself. An out-of-date book bearing an old-fashioned title: *How To Please The Him In Your Life*. Quite out of pace with today's how-to-be-a-successful-woman books. She had seen it on a dusty shelf in a used book store and found it amusing. As if anyone would go to all this trouble, trying to please a man!

Oh, well, it was in line with her old-fashioned ideas, wasn't it? Maybe she should see if it worked. She thumbed through the pages and found the most unlikely, though most pertinent at the moment, advice. "What To Feed Him When He Needs A Pickup."

Scot awoke to the sound of a cheerful, "It's ready. Come and get it," and an appetizing aroma drifting from the kitchen. He followed his nose to a prettily set table, and sat down to a delicious repast. Chicken so tender he could cut it with his fork, spicy apple slices, fluffy creamed potatoes, green peas and carrots. Not his usual fare, but . . .

"Very tasty," he said. "But I feel a little guilty. I was sleeping and you were still working."

"I haven't just returned from a trip to Denver and a long meeting last night. You deserve a break. Anyone who handles the heavy load you have needs all the help he can get."

"Why, thank you, ma'am. I'm glad you realize it."

"Oh, stop that grinning! I really do like the way you operate, and it burns me up when you're saddled with silly details that others should..." She stopped. "Okay, I guess I got a little miffed at Reba tonight, but, to tell the truth, I'm glad you took over that little detail. Otherwise, a young boy might have missed a chance he needs."

Scot was warmed by her words and the gleam of genuine admiration in her eyes. "I wonder where Reba will place him," he mused.

"I think I'll ask her to give him to us," Lisa said. "Start him at the top. I sure learned the business running errands for the head shed."

"You sure did," he said. And meant it. The best assistant he ever had. "And you can cook, too," he added.

"I'm learning," she said, smiling. "Part of the preparation, you know."

"Preparation?"

"For marriage."

That jolted him. "Good Lord! Are you still on that kick?"

"Certainly. Does that surprise you? We covered my agenda pretty thoroughly in that first interview, didn't we?"

"Well...er...I suppose. Only..." He had only half believed it in the first place, and, most of the time, forgot about it. And, anyway hadn't thought... "Look, I said it then and I'll say it again. People don't prepare for marriage. At least not until they fall in love with some special somebody."

"I know." She speared an apple slice and popped it into her mouth. "That's sad, isn't it?"

"Sad?"

"To base your life on love."

"Miss Wilson!" he said in exaggerated shock. "How can you demean the most profound force on earth? Love ye one another, sayeth the—"

"Oh, sure. Universally. But we're talking the personal Adam and Eve force."

"Which is different?"

"And dangerous."

"Oh?"

"One could get caught," she explained to his raised brow, "by good looks or glands or most any little thing."

"Equally insignificant, I presume?"

"Oh, you needn't smirk! Think about it," she said, pointing with her fork. "There you are, enchanted by a pair of dreamy blue eyes or full of goose bumps from the touch of strong, bulging muscles, and...bingo! Before you know it, you are stuck with a muscular penny pincher who dotes on country-western instead of the free-spending Bach lover you'd much prefer. Or vice versa. He finds the body beautiful can't cook. Okay, laugh!'' She handed another napkin to Scot, who was choking on his coffee. ''Slightly exaggerated, but you do see what I mean, don't you?''

He nodded, coughed, and when he could speak, said, ''You do make a point. But...stuck? Mistakes can be remedied. Divorce is—''

''Messy and complicated, especially if there are children. Also, a big waste of time.''

''And expensive,'' he agreed, thinking of his brother. ''So perhaps there is method to your madness,'' he conceded. ''So you are prepared for that mysterious Mr. Right?''

''Oh, never! As you know, premiums must be paid, or the policy will lapse.'' She grinned. ''It's an ongoing process, you see. Speaking of which, we'd better get going.''

She sure seems prepared, he thought as he watched her clear the table. Quite different from the gopher who had brought his morning coffee and watered the plants. Still does, come to think of it. But she was...different. Or maybe he had gotten to know her better. Found out she could cook, play golf, and was...well, fun to be with, at work or play. And looking at her now, in that frilly wraparound thing she had changed into... Damn! Glands! Better watch it, buddy.

"Okay, boss. Back to the grindstone."

He looked at the folders she placed before him, then back at her. It had been a long time since that first interview, and everything about her, her looks, her whole demeanor, had changed. What he had thought remote now loomed as an imminent possibility. The thought disturbed him. Those roses... "Do you have someone in mind?" he asked.

"Well." She tapped her pencil against her lips. "What do you think of Joe Prescott?"

"Huh?"

"Or Danville. He knows the area pretty well."

He stared at her.

"You were thinking of who should arrange the West Coast Regional, weren't you?"

"Er... Oh. Sure. Prescott. Good choice." He bent to the work before him, and didn't refer to the question until they had finished. However, it still bugged him, and when she began to close folders, he asked again. Casually. Joking. "So. Have you found him?"

"Who?"

"This paragon. The Mr. Right you keep harping about."

"Oh." Her laugh was low and musical. "I'm not sure." He was still pondering on this unassuring answer as she continued, "All finished and not yet ten o'clock. Not bad. Now you may have a treat.''

"A treat?"

"I suppose you noticed I served no wine or dessert.''

"No." He hadn't even thought about it.

"Well, I didn't. They inhibit the thinking process."

"Really? And where do you get all these gems of wisdom?"

"From a little manual I found on a deserted book shelf."

"I see." But he wasn't thinking of manuals or gems. Only of the sparkle of laughter in her eyes, the perfect outline of lush parted lips, the slender throat and delicate curves so invitingly revealed by a loosely wrapped wraparound.

"So what is your preference, sir? Cake or wine . . . Brandy? Something sweet or something stimulating?"

"Both," he whispered, crushing her to him and closing his mouth on those luscious lips. Oh, yes! So sweet. A sensation sizzling through him with a charge, electric and effervescent, like a potent drink for which he had long thirsted. He had to quench the thirst. Over and over again he tasted the sweetness of her lips, traced the firm slender lines of her body, the soft curves beneath the sheer garment, breathed in the fragrance of her. He lost count of time. Had no thought or reason.

Only feeling. He wanted it to last forever. Still holding her close, he lifted his head to look down at her; she stared at him with wide startled eyes. But she did not pull away. And he remembered that there had been no resistance. Not once. Only the precious yielding of that sweet body pressed close to his, a hand clutching his chest, her mouth against the hollow of his throat. He felt a surge of pure delight and lightly touched his mouth to hers.

"This is... Isn't... Not right," her lips whispered against his.

"Why?" he whispered back.

"Not... not good business."

"No." To hell with business. He peppered her face with kisses.

"Oh... Please...!"

"Please what?" he coaxed, his tongue tasting the lobe of her ear. She gave a moan of pleasure so potently stimulating that he continued to tease and probe, to—

"Oh, no! Please..." This time the plea was as much protest as pleasure. "Wait! This... Glands!"

"Yes." He felt the powerful surge in his groin.

"Stop!"

He didn't want to stop.

With a strength unbelievable in so small a figure, she pushed him away. "You shouldn't... I shouldn't. It's all my fault."

"Yes." She shouldn't be so temptingly beautiful. So... He reached for her.

She backed away. "I didn't mean to... Well, you know. Glands can get you in trouble."

Scot sat in his car, not daring to switch on the engine. Not until he had gained some control.

Damn! Damn! Damn!

Never had he been so firmly rejected. Dismissed. Tossed...no, kicked out!

Okay...a gentle kick. Apologizing all over the place. "Sorry. All my fault. I shouldn't have let...made this happen." When she knew darn well it was he who reached for her.

But she hadn't resisted, had she?

Not one damn bit! Just the opposite. Nestled in his arms like she meant to stay forever... With him all the way, yielding to the same mounting, all-consuming passion, so powerful it still held him in its grip. And then, right in the midst...stop!

He didn't understand.

Oh, the hell with it! He switched on the engine. Halfway to his condo, his car phone buzzed.

Lisa! He eagerly reached for the phone.

"Scot! At last," came a voice from the past.

"Hello, Gwen," he said, swallowing the disappointment. When was the last time he had seen Gwen Bradley?

"It's been ages and ages," she supplied. "Much too long. I've been trying to catch you, but I know you power brokers...busy, busy, busy. So I forgive you. Why don't you stop by now?"

"At this hour?"

"Not too late for...a nightcap."

"Well..." Why the hell not?

Because he didn't want to see Gwen Bradley, or anybody except... "Thanks, but no. Not tonight. I've just had a tough session." Damn tough! "Another time, maybe?"

He turned the car toward his club. He'd work out. Take a long swim.

CHAPTER TEN

"GOOD morning, boss!" Same lilting voice, sunny smile. "Your coffee, sir." As if last night...

He stood up. "Lisa, about last night—"

"I know. Not good business."

"I wasn't thinking about business."

"Neither of us was. A big mistake. Please..." She hesitated, a look of desperation in her eyes. "Couldn't we just...just forget it?"

"We could."

"Thank you," she said gratefully, looking relieved. "Now... I've relayed your instructions and set everything in motion. Only..." She went on to explain a problem and possible solutions. She talked rapidly, moving her head in that intense way. The sun streaming through the big window glistened on the flecks of gold in her hair. Her dress was a plain brown sheath, loosely fitted, concealing. So how did it hint so temptingly of the soft curves beneath?

"Mistakes can be repeated," he said.

Her head jerked up to face him directly. "Or avoided."

"Are you sure about that?"

"Quite. I like my job, Mr. Harding." She consulted her notes. "The West Coast Regional. You did settle on Prescott?"

"Yes. Prescott," he said.

"All my fault," Lisa explained to Mary Wells that afternoon. "You see I had been reading this book..."

"What book?"

"On how to please the man in your life."

"Honey, you don't need a book for that."

"I do. I don't have your want-to-get-married club."

Mary laughed. "Start one. There must be lots of women who want to get married."

"None I know. Meaningful relationship, maybe. And just as a sideline to what they're really working on...like a career."

"I see. Rather, I don't. In my day..." She shook her head. "Hand me that trowel. So you got this book and it's no good, either?"

"Oh, it's so ridiculous, you can't take it seriously. But..." She gave her the trowel. "What it says works, Mary. It really does."

"So what went wrong?"

"Well, last night, I was working with Mr. Harding, my boss. At my place." She paused. "That was the first mistake. But I suggested, took him there because I was concerned about him."

"Oh."

"He's a don't-know-when-to-stop workaholic, Mary. He's one of these ladder climbers, you see, and—"

"Ladder climbers?"

"Oh, you know, one of those people so anxious to get ahead that..." She hesitated. "No. Maybe that's the wrong term for him. He is ambitious, but not for himself. More for what needs to be done. For the right things, even down to the smallest detail. Even last night. There was this boy that had got into trouble and... Oh, never mind about that. The thing is, I could tell he was overtaxed, hungry, and we still had so much to do. So I thought if I fed him... at my place where it was quiet."

"That was thoughtful of you," Mary said as she dug around the tomato plants.

"I guess. I fed him just what the book said was a pickup, and it was. We got through in record time."

"Good. So you had the right idea."

"Only maybe I was wrong. You see, something else happened." Lisa, who had changed into a pair of her old shorts, got down beside Mary and began to pull out weeds. "You know, I changed my whole wardrobe, per advice from the stylist at Hera's. Tailored for the office, sexy at home."

"Well?"

"Well, I didn't want to cook in my office clothes, so I'd changed into the first thing I put my hands on when I got home."

"And?"

Lisa sat back, looking thoughtful. "One of those when-you-want-to-entice-him garments."

"Oh, my!" Mary exclaimed, laughing. "And did it?"

Lisa made a face. "I'll say. We were through work, just relaxing, you know. Suddenly he looked at me like he'd never seen me before and then . . . Well, all of a sudden he was kissing me like crazy. Or maybe it was me kissing him, because I was feeling like I never wanted him to stop. It was so . . . so . . ."

"Wonderful, huh?"

"Yes. Oh, no! Awful!"

"Oh?" Mary looked puzzled. "Sounds as if you liked it."

"That's just it, don't you see? Dangerous. I could be drawn into a purely physical relationship with the wrong man."

"Oh. He's married?"

"No."

"A playboy type?"

"No. At least . . . I don't think so." She started pulling weeds again, thinking about it. There were women who called or sometimes stopped by the office. But she really didn't know how or with whom he spent what little spare time he had.

"How does he feel about you?" Mary asked.

She didn't know that, either. Hadn't thought about it, even when he was kissing her. Too involved with her own feelings then. "That doesn't matter, Mary. He's just not a man I'd want to marry."

"Why not? From what you said, he's nice, hardworking."

"That's just it." She stopped. How could she explain about work versus family time? Not to Mary whose hardworking Horace had had very little time for family life during his working years. "He...he's not my type."

"I see," said the obviously puzzled Mary.

"Besides, he's my boss! That makes situations like last night extremely awkward. This morning... Oh, Mary it was awful! I tried to appear normal, but I could hardly face him."

"I can imagine. Do you think he'll fire you? Some bosses, I hear, are—"

"No. He's not like that."

"Oh. Well, are you going to quit?"

"I can't quit! I'm up to my ears. I have finished paying for that beauty course. But keeping up...manicures, facials...you can't imagine. And those what-to-wear-when clothes don't come cheap." She sighed. "No, I'll have to keep my well-paying job till it happens."

"Until what happens?"

"Until I get married of course. That's what I've been working for all the time. The beauty treatments, the book, clothes, everything...even why I took the job in the first place."

"That's right. You told me. So when do you think...that is, have you found the...the right type?"

"Do you know," she said dreamily. "I really think I have." Jake Mason. Maybe...

Yes, Scot thought, mistakes could and should be avoided. Office affairs were strictly taboo. Should he lose the best assistant he ever had because he found her physically appealing?

Not on your life!

If he could vacation with her all over East Africa and avoid troublesome episodes, surely he could travel, work with her anywhere, couldn't he?

Bet your life he could!

Anyway, he'd probably been working too hard. Too close?

Possibly.

Distractions were available.

If the distractions weren't entirely satisfactory, at least they were...distracting. And, at the office, if he kept his mind and eyes strictly on the business at hand, operations at Safetech's head shed sailed on smooth, undistracted waters.

Lisa was no longer wary. Things were really back to normal. As far as she could tell, Scot Harding regarded her as no more than a piece of necessary office equipment. That, she told herself, was a big relief. If at times, most unexpectedly, she felt a little quiver or a hot flush at the sight of some now familiar sight . . . his rumpled head bent over a stack of papers or just that funny quizzical lift of one eyebrow . . . it was, she told herself, just glands. And was comforted by the thought that the present situation wouldn't last forever. Jake . . .

She concentrated on Jake, the ideal husband material. Semiretired, with all the time in the world for family life. More than enough money to supply the glamour. More important, she liked him. He was an affable, easygoing, delightful companion, when boating, golfing, dancing . . . whatever.

And he liked her. She could tell. His attentions had increased, the invitations numerous and more expansive. "How about sailing to Hawaii?" or "A flight on the Concorde? We could sail back on the *Q.E. II*."

Strangely enough, none of his fantastic suggestions seemed particularly exciting to her. She always gave her usual calm, truthful answer. "Sorry. I'm a working girl."

But now his response was, "You don't have to be a working girl."

She wasn't dumb. He didn't necessarily mean marriage. She would wait.

Meanwhile, she set her own standards. She was not about to accompany him on any intimate sojourn without a wedding ring on her—

"Here's what you wanted from Fiscal, Miss Wilson."

"Thank you, Jefrey." She smiled at Jefrey Fisher, the young intern Reba had gladly assigned to her. He didn't look like a juvenile delinquent. He looked like an ordinary sixteen-year-old of average height, skinny, with freckles and red hair. Possibly more enthusiastic than most, she thought as she studied his obviously awed expression.

"Man, that's some place," he said. "All them computers and people punching buttons and numbers jumping up... bip, bop, bam! I'd like to... can you work those things, Miss Wilson?"

"Oh, yes, I did so every day, and not too long ago. Word processing, though. I'm not very good at figures."

"I am. That was the only class I... Well, I got pretty good grades in math, even algebra. And if'n I'd had one of them computers I'd been a whiz. The machine does all the figuring. You don't have to think."

"Oh, yes, you do. You know what they say... garbage in, garbage out."

"You mean...oh, like you have to put in what to subtract or multiply or whatever. Heck, that's easy. I could do that."

"I expect you could. You're a pretty smart young man, Jefrey. Listen, take these over to Personnel, and when you come back..." She was aware of the proud lift of his head and his careful attention to what she was saying. It was a joy to have such an eager, anxious-to-learn young helper. She was glad they had taken him on, she thought as she watched him go out.

She was unaware that Harding, standing in the doorway of his adjoining office, also watched. She was surprised when he spoke.

"Have you made the reservations for the West Coast Regional?"

"Not yet. I've alerted Travel, but—"

"Good. Get a ticket and book a room for Jefrey."

"But..." She gave him a quizzical look that asked why.

"I want him to be the conference page."

"A good idea. I never thought of that."

"I find him to be unusually curious, intellectually. So not only will this give him a chance to perform the necessary functions of a page, but an excellent opportunity to see and observe."

She agreed, smiling.

"I like that. And it's good for him. Do you know that all that kid has ever seen in his life are the streets of Wilmington? And not the best streets at that.''

''Yes,'' she said again, surprised that she had never thought about that.

''He's a bright kid and the more he sees of the working world, the better. I'll speak to Glover and his parole officer.'' Harding started to go into his office, then turned back. ''Arrange for us to stay over one more day. Maybe we'll take in Disneyland. He needs to know that working has its fun benefits, as well.''

He went back into his office, and Lisa sat for a long time in contemplation. How many men, beset with the responsibilities and problems inherent in such an empire as Harding headed, would have had the interest or taken the time . . .

Then she thought of Jefrey. He would be out of his gourd. She must impress upon him his own responsibility . . . behavior, attire. Attire. She would see about getting him fitted for a Safetech uniform. Right away. The conference was only ten days away. He might need other things. Perhaps she should arrange for a pay advance. No, travel advance. That would do it.

CHAPTER ELEVEN

WHY, Jefrey looks positively handsome, Lisa thought when she came down to registration that first morning of the conference. Very correct in the Safetech uniform...blue slacks and blazer with the discreet Safetech emblem on its pocket. Light blue shirt, distinctive tie.

He stood by the registration desk, looking quite professional, though a bit anxious. She had tried to reassure him. "It will be easy. Just be alert for whatever is needed. Mostly you'll be asked to run errands, answer phone calls, hand out materials...things like that."

"But what if I can't...don't know where to go or something?"

"Oh, you will. You'll be given directions, locations...probably a dry run the night before. You'll be fine. Just act as you do here...smile as if you're glad to be helpful."

He didn't need that latter advice, she thought now, watching him as closely as a coach would a protégé. Jefrey was always eager to do what was asked, anxious to please. Almost as if he knew this was a great, unbelievable, maybe last chance, and he didn't want to muff it.

No. It was more than that. No one could mistake the awe, the wonder, as he took in a world he had never seen before.

Even the plane ride. "Have you flown before?" she asked.

He shook his head, and she could tell he was too overwhelmed to speak. But not too overwhelmed to enjoy it. During most of the flight, she had been absorbed, reviewing pertinent details with Scot. But she had been aware of Jefrey. Gaping out the window, ordering dozens of sodas and fiddling with his private TV afforded by the first-class status.

And now the plush, elegant hotel. His own private room with all the amenities. She watched him smile and nod, and supply an elder gentleman with a pen and memo pad, then go quickly out to deliver the message. As if it was a treat to do what was asked. As if he was proud to be part of this mass of elegant professional people who spoke respectfully to him, requesting that he do this or that.

She looked over at Scot, deeply involved in a discussion with Prescott. All business, just as on the plane. As if he had no thought of Jefrey nor of the opportunities he had made possible for him.

It was a three-day conference, and a busy one. Lisa soon became so involved in her own duties that she forgot all about Jefrey. Thursday was particularly grueling, and she retired to her room immediately after the evening session. One more day, she thought as she climbed into bed.

Too keyed up to sleep, she turned on the bedside lamp and reached for a paperback.

The phone rang. Almost twelve. Who on earth? she wondered as she answered.

"Hello, doll. Conference going well?"

"Oh, Jake! How nice to hear from you. Yes, going well. Only one more day."

"Good," he said. "I miss you."

"Me, too." She forgave the lie. Not kind to say she had forgotten to think about him.

"So what time are you landing Saturday?"

"Saturday? Oh, I'm not! Sunday at—"

"Why not? You are finishing up tomorrow?"

"Yes, but we arranged to stay over a day."

"Who's we?" Jake sounded annoyed. "You and Scot?"

"Yes. And Jefrey."

"Who's Jefrey?"

"He's a young intern that works in our office. He's serving as a page during the conference. A really bright, nice kid. He's been working real hard. And Scot…Mr. Harding, thought it would be nice for him to have some fun. And since we're here…you know…Disneyland."

"I see. Well…you could take an earlier flight, couldn't you? You don't have to stay."

"Oh, but..." She stopped. How to explain that she wanted to stay? Wanted to see Jefrey having fun. "Hard to change a reservation on such short notice."

"I assure you, sweetheart, that it can be done. Wait. I've a better idea. I'll have Conyers pick you up."

"Conyers?"

"One of the pilots. He'll bring the jet down and—"

"Jake, don't be ridiculous!" She hadn't yet grasped the idea of one having one's own private jet on command at any moment. "I already have a ticket and it's only one day."

"But I want you here so we can go sailing on Sunday. I thought we might—"

"For goodness' sake, we are always... that is, we can go sailing anytime."

"No, we can't. You're always working. Which reminds me, it's time we did something about that."

"Oh?"

"We'll talk about it when I see you. Which will be in about twenty-four hours, would you say? I'll have Conyers..."

"No, Jake. Don't do that. It's... well, I promised Jefrey." She crossed her fingers. "He'll be disappointed if I don't go with him."

"Oh, so the little jerk means more to you than I?"

"Don't be silly. It's just...well, a promise is a promise."

"Okay. I'll try to survive. But you do realize how long it's been?"

"At least four days. Ages," she said with mock emphasis.

"So have you been dreaming?"

"Dreaming?"

"Sweet little dreams of me!"

"Why, Mr. Mason, you shouldn't delve into a woman's silly romantic notions!"

"Oh, but I must. Such notions are to be shared," he admonished in a seductive whisper. "Hold on to them, sweetheart. Till I'm with you to make them come true."

"I'm holding! I'm holding!" she panted.

"Nut. Good night, love."

Lisa was laughing as she replaced the phone. I like Jake, she thought. I am really very fond of him, she added, somewhat firmly, as she retrieved the paperback.

The conference ended late Friday afternoon. Harding had a wrap-up session with Prescott and some other officials that evening. He hadn't stopped one minute, Lisa thought, and was glad he had planned the Disneyland trip. He needed the relaxation more than Jefrey, who, along with other pages and clerks, was sorting and packaging materials to be transported to various offices.

They were seated at breakfast early the next morning, excitedly going over the brochures, planning what to see, what to do, when—

"Aha, I thought I'd find you here. Fortifying yourselves for the big adventure?"

Lisa stared at Jake, tall, slim, and handsome in designer jeans and polo shirt, looking as mischievous as a small boy who had just pulled off a big joke on somebody. Which he had.

She was suddenly unaccountably angry. Why had he come?

"Jake!" It was Harding, as surprised as she, who asked, "What are you doing here?"

But it was to Lisa that Jake responded. "If the mountain won't come to Mohammed," he said, and bent to kiss her full on the lips.

It was not the impact of the kiss, but the expression on Scot's face that made her go all hot and cold...intense and demanding, forcing her to remember *his* kiss. A kiss that had shaken her to the roots. Was he remembering, too?

She forced herself to look away, feeling awkward as she turned to Jake. "What...what a nice surprise!" she said, smiling, wondering why she felt he was an intruder. "When did you get here?"

"Too late last night to disturb you," he said, sitting next to her and helping himself to one of her strawberries, a gesture as possessive as his kiss and just as embarrassing. "Since you couldn't go sailing with me, I decided to go Disneylanding with you."

"Amazed that you could tear yourself from the pressures of...the golf course," Scot remarked, tight-lipped.

"Difficult," Jake replied with complacent good cheer. "But the thought of Lisa in the company of..." He hesitated, rather belatedly casting a glance at Jefrey. "Two charming gentlemen for such long hours—"

"A daily occurrence," Scot said. "That disturbs you?"

"Oh, not at all. Not at all. Work can be so boring, you see. But when it comes to play or other pastimes—"

"Jake," Lisa broke in, "this is Jefrey, the young man I told you about. Jefrey, this is Mr. Mason. He's...going to join us, I hope," she added, with a questioning smile toward Jake.

"That's what I came for. So, Jefrey, I understand you're a recent addition to the Safetech staff. How do you like it?"

Lisa was glad to see him focus his attention on Jefrey and cease the bickering—was it bickering?—with Scot. She knew they were the best of friends and that day golfing, when she had met Jake, they seemed to make it a game...well, to cap on each other. But today... Somehow the atmosphere had changed.

Or maybe it was she. Why did she feel kind of...deflated? Since Jake had come. Like the day was something she and Scot had planned together for Jefrey, and Jake had no business ...

This was ridiculous. Jake always made things more fun. Besides, he was the man she was going to marry. That is, if he asked her.

But would she?

Could she promise to love him? Did she?

A marriage could be planned. But love? Not something that could be forced. It had to come naturally, like breathing, didn't it?

Or maybe it had to grow. She liked Jake. And he had come all this way just to be with her, hadn't he? She touched his hand. "I'm so glad you came."

The tension, if indeed there had been tension, had eased by the time they reached Disneyland. The happy jostling crowd, the atmosphere, all there was to see and do, affected all of them. How could one not play in a playground such as this? Joking and laughing like four kids on a holiday, they set out to try everything. They walked through every level of the massive tree house, took three harrowing rides down Magic Mountain, and several tumbles down the giant waterfall. They rode through the ghost house, visited Tom Sawyer's island, took a canoe ride through jungle waters infested with very real-looking alligators and hippos, consumed dozens

of hot dogs, hamburgers, and gallons of sodas
in cool, clean tree-shaded restaurants. They got
stymied at Space Mountain where Jefrey insisted
on at least eight breathtaking rides through the
darkened star-studded area of simulated space.

"You really get the feeling like you're way out
among the stars, don't you?" she said to Jake,
who, after the third ride, waited with her on a
nearby bench. "I don't know if I really got dizzy
or was just overwhelmed by the idea of being so
far from good old solid earth. I'm sorry I had
to give up on Jefrey."

"I'm not." Jake reached for her hand. "It's
time I had you to myself."

"Jake, I've been with you all day."

"All to myself," he emphasized. "Listen,
you're flying back with me."

"Okay. I think Jefrey's really enjoying this,
don't you?"

"Are you kidding! We might never leave this
Space Mountain."

"Isn't that the truth! I'm glad Scot's sticking
with him." Going all out for Jefrey, she thought.
But seeming to enjoy it just as much. Funny how
at times Scot would shed that all business at-
titude as easily as he did his coat. Like when they
toured in Africa, and that night they went
dancing in San Francisco, even, she thought,
feeding Clarice's kids. She smiled, remembering.
"Open up, kid."

"Would you like that?" Jake asked, kissing her cheek.

"I'm...er...not sure," she muttered, wondering what he had asked.

"We'd get to Wilmington about four, probably...but we wouldn't have to budge till breakfast. Then we could head straight for the boat."

"Oh, Jake, you move too fast for me," she said, trying to gather her thoughts. Leave tonight? Sleep on his plane, which, if she knew Jake, was cozily fitted with a full-size bed. Not a good idea. "There's no telling when we will get away from here, and I'm already exhausted. And I haven't even packed. We'd better plan to leave in the morning." She looked down at her watch, then up at the Space Mountain. How long? she wondered.

Scot, trapped in the capsule for his sixth—or was it the seventh—hurtle through the simulated areas of a vast outer world, wondered the same thing. He wondered how long it would be before space travel became as common as a plane flight. He wondered where Lisa was. With Jake. Very chummy. Too damn chummy. He wondered how long that had been going on. He didn't like it. He knew Jake. A good enough guy, but careless with his charm and his millions, leaving a trail of broken hearts. Lisa, for all the veneer of sophistication she assumed, was a very naive

young woman. Warm, caring, honest.
Vulnerable.

He didn't like it one damn bit!

Lisa enjoyed the flight to Wilmington in Jake's
plane. She was right. Not just a bed, but a whole
comfortable, beautifully furnished bedroom. An
equally comfortable living room.

"Such luxury," she said. "A person could be
spoiled."

"I like spoiling you," he said. "What would
you like? Coffee? Breakfast? A nap?"

"Goodness, no. I slept all night, and I had my
fruit and coffee at the hotel. I think I'll just relax
and enjoy all this and heaven, too. It's beautiful,"
she said, gazing out at cliffs and clouds.

"You're beautiful," he said, running a finger
along the ruffled collar of her orchid blouse. "I
like this. So soft and frilly and just right for you."

She smiled at him. "The better to entice you,
sir."

"Are you trying to entice me?"

"You bet your life I am!"

"Come here. Let me show you how."

She moved closer to him. He kissed her.
Slowly, tenderly. She was not enticed. She pressed
close, trying to respond. Nothing.

She looked up at his handsome face, deeply
bronzed against his blond sun-bleached hair. An

outdoor man...sailing, golfing. What was he really like?

"Tell me about yourself," she said. "Your parents. Are they living?"

"Both. Divorced. Mom's in Paris. Dad in New York." He ran his fingers through her hair. "I think I'm falling in love."

She wasn't ready to hear this. "You're changing the subject," she said, sitting up.

"Come back to me."

"No. You're cheating. You're supposed to tell me all about you. Did you have a happy childhood or were you a poor little neglected rich boy? Did you have nannies or tutors that gave you a complex?"

He grinned. "No complex. And never neglected. Not a chance, what with parents, grandparents, uncles, aunts, and several cousins."

She, who had been left with just one aunt, sighed. "All those relatives. More precious than money."

"That's debatable," he said with a wry smile. "But, since you think so...would you like to join?"

"Join what?"

"The family."

"How do I do that?"

"You marry me, goose!"

"Oh. I..." There it was. Just like that. He had asked her. "Stop kidding," she hedged.

"I've never been so serious in my life." He took her hand, rubbed his thumb over her ring finger. "I've had a few relationships, Lisa. One or two very close ones. But I've never before asked anyone to marry me."

"Oh, Jake." She touched his cheek. "I feel so...so touched, honored. You are special. I'm really fond of you. But marriage...is serious. I'll... Could I have time...to think about it?"

"All the time you want. I can wait."

Why was she waiting? He was perfect, exactly the kind of man she wanted. So why did she hesitate?

Because she truly liked Jake. He was a dear man. He deserved a woman who really loved him.

She wasn't sure that she could be that woman.

CHAPTER TWELVE

THE trouble, Lisa reflected, once she gained the solitude of her apartment, was that she had had no experience with a close man/woman relationship. That had not particularly bothered her. Her teen years, despite the braces, had been okay—part of the happy crowd that always gathered at the Wells's house. But she had not been one of the pretty sought-after girls, and anyway, the Wells boys had been as protective as they were bullying. So she had missed out on the usual teenage experimental petting . . . kissing.

After she was on her own?

Well, she hadn't exactly been overloaded with dates. Until Jake.

To tell the truth, she felt toward Jake as she would a good-natured, likable brother. Maybe after living so long with the Wells boys, she had a tendency to treat all men like brothers.

All men?

She swallowed, remembering. Scot. He didn't seem . . . feel . . . anything like a brother. Sometimes, just looking at him, she got a peculiar woozy sensation. A melting almost as powerful as when he kissed her.

Glands. A natural reaction, she had thought, between any man and woman who became . . . well, close.

Maybe this was the time to consult the sex manuals.

They told how. So specifically that just the reading made her blush.

But all the manuals dwelt on the sex act itself, not the preamble leading to it. Nothing about the magic sensation, that electric jolt of passionate yearning that impelled the romance heroine to strip off her clothes and fly into her lover's arms for a mutually satisfying orgy. The way a wife ought to feel about her husband.

The way she felt when Scot kissed her.

She wouldn't think about that.

Scot's regular early Sunday morning golf foursome was more often a three or twosome, dependant upon who was presently in town. This morning it was a twosome, just he and Jake Mason. He was glad about that. He wanted to talk to Jake.

He didn't waste time. "I was sure surprised when you popped up in L.A. last week."

"Oh? Well, you know me." Jake shrugged. "Hey, aren't those new woods?"

"Yeah. I didn't know you and Lisa were an item. How long has that been going on?"

"Lisa? Oh, I don't know. Since...hey, you introduced us. You asked me to get Senator Dobbs down and..."

"Right. I remember." Big damn mistake!

"Custom-made, huh?" Jake's eyes were on the clubs. "Let me have a look."

Scot handed over a club while his mind grappled with something else. Jake might be his best friend, but how the hell could he pursue a subject that was none of his damn business?

Jake ran a hand over the smooth wood, looked at the label. "Leonard, huh?"

Scot nodded.

"He's good. Great sticks." Jake handed back the club. "Won't help you, though. I'm out for blood today."

"You'll probably get it. As usual. But if I had as much time to play as you..." That reminded him. "What happened to Gloria?"

"Who?" Jake looked so genuinely puzzled that Scot shook his head.

"Gloria somebody," he said with emphasis. "Surely you remember. The gorgeous redhead you squired all over the continent last year."

"Oh, her! She was gorgeous, wasn't she? I think she's in Hollywood. At least, I got her a contract with one of the networks. But I don't know where she is. She sort of faded out of my life."

"Or you faded out of hers?"

They were approaching the tee. Jake stopped and turned to give him a level look. "What are you driving at, Scot?"

"No offense. But you do have a love-'em-leave-'em reputation, you know."

"So?"

"Lisa Wilson's different."

"I'll say."

"Not your type."

"I'll buy that." They had reached the tee and were standing a little apart waiting for the foursome before them to tee off. "Lisa's nobody's type."

"Right. She's for real."

Jake met his clear unwavering stare without blinking. "What are you saying?"

"That she wouldn't be bought off with a contract, a condo, diamond bracelets. Nothing like that."

"I know. I've tried."

Scot felt a sense of elation. His faith in Lisa was justified. She wouldn't fall for Jake Mason's maneuvering. Would not be influenced by his charm or his millions.

"Why the inquisition?" Jake asked.

"I like her. I wouldn't want her hurt."

"I see. Are you asking my intentions?"

That floored him. He had never known Jake to have but one intention...for whoever captured his fancy at the moment. "I . . . I guess I am."

The answer struck him like a bolt of lightning. "Strictly honorable, old friend."

"Meaning?"

"That I mean to marry the lady. Satisfied?"

"No, by God, I'm not!" A swinging bachelor like Jake? "You'd make a hell of a husband."

"Not exactly asking your permission, chum."

"What?"

"You're her employer, remember? Not her father."

"Yes, but—"

"Besides which . . . any father would consider me a most desirable catch."

Scot stared at him. Yes. Most fathers would. And so would Lisa.

Damn! Damn! Damn!

I am the fool. A stupid, blundering moron. Worried about poor naive vulnerable Lisa . . . who knew exactly what she was doing.

He should have been protecting Jake. Poor old love-'em-leave-'em Jake, who didn't know he was dealing with bait.

Yes, sir. Lisa had set herself up as bait and she had caught the big fish!

Well, bully for her!

"Get a move on, man. We're on," Jake prompted and Scot saw that the foursome had moved on.

"Right!" Scot strode over and set up his ball and took out his wood. Swung. The resounding whack sent the ball spinning far down the fairway.

"Damn!" Jake said. "You're the one out for blood!"

"Guess what, Miss Wilson? I been moved to a new place."

"That's good." Lisa looked up from her desk. Must be a good move, judging by the grin on Jefrey's face.

"Yeah. This is the best place I ever been. A whole room all by myself."

"That's nice."

"Yeah, just us four boys in the big house and we all got our own room."

Lisa frowned. No adult? "Just you boys?"

"Oh, no. It's Mr. and Mrs. Johnson's house. He teaches math, but she don't work. See, they run this moter...moter...some kind of program."

"Motivation program?"

"Yeah, that's it. Mr. Glover got me in it on account of me working here, and Mr. Harding says I can work part time even after school starts. See, that's the kind of program it is. They learn you to do some kind of work."

"You learn. Others teach, or train you."

"Yeah. That's what they do. And Mr. Harding, he give me this computer—"

"Gave you."

"Yeah, and I'm gonna learn how to do those figures like they do in Fiscal. Mr. Harding says that's where he's going to put me on account of I'm good at math. I like it here, but he says I don't want to be a gopher all my life." He paused, looking puzzled. "What's a gopher, Miss Wilson?"

She smiled. "Just an expression people have coined. You know how you run errands...go for this or go for that?"

"Oh, yeah." Jefrey grinned. "So pretty soon I'll be sitting at a desk and somebody else'll be the gopher, huh?"

"Right," Lisa said, thinking of Jefrey working with figures at a computer. Because Scot Harding had an eye for details. He had noted that Jefrey was good at math, just as he had known she would be good at what she was doing now. "Mr. Harding is pretty proud of you, Jefrey. That's because you have carried out your duties so well here, and conducted yourself like a gentleman. I'm proud of you, too, and I hate to lose you. But this is a promotion, you know, and I'm glad for you. Just keep up the good work." She didn't add "and out of trouble," but he seemed to sense the admonition.

"I am. I'm going to work hard, and I ain't gonna miss no more school, and I ain't gonna do nothing that Mr. Harding wouldn't like."

"Good. Oh, good morning, boss." She looked up, smiling, as Harding strode in.

He only gave them a curt nod, and went straight into his office.

"Take this packet to Mr. Alexander," she told Jefrey. "And I better get Mr. Harding's coffee." She liked to make him comfortable. Somebody should look after him. He was always so busy, so rushed. Always observing and alert to what was needed for anything or anybody else. Whatever section of the business, whatever country he was dealing with, whatever person. He had known before she did that she would be good at·her job. She was good. And, to tell the truth, she liked it.

Not that she meant to be trapped in it! No, indeed. As soon as she got married, probably a few weeks before she got married, she would resign. Maybe she should alert him now. So he could be looking around for a replacement.

She went quickly in with his coffee . . . hot, just as he liked it. "Here's your coffee, boss!" She smiled and took out her notepad. "Let's see. Fiscal meeting at ten. Do you want me to cover it? You have an eleven-thirty luncheon with Davis at Perry's and . . ." She stopped. He wasn't listening. He was staring at her as if he had something else on his mind. Something not very pleasant.

"Congratulations, Miss Wilson."

"Con...? For what, pray tell?"

"Pulled it off, didn't you?"

She stiffened, not liking the way he was looking at her. "I don't know what you're talking about."

"I'm talking about manipulation, Miss Wilson."

"Manipulation?"

"I'm talking about your setting yourself up as bait."

"Bait?"

"Bait. I think I arranged a loan to assist you in that nefarious scheme."

Now she remembered. That first interview when he had goaded her into telling her plans. He had called it marriage bait. "It was not a nefarious scheme."

"Oh? Are you denying that you deliberately planned to attract a man... No, how did you put it? A certain type of man. A rich type... not so involved with making a living that he wouldn't have time to make a marriage."

"No. I'm not denying it." Now she was really angry. He had pulled it out of her, but she had been honest. And why was he bringing it up now? "That is the type... the kind of man I want to marry."

"Found him, didn't you?"

He must be talking about Jake. "Maybe," she said through tight lips.

"Plenty rich. Not an old retired fogy, either. Still young enough to make babies, huh?"

She bit her lip, trying to control her temper. "Okay. So I'm lucky. Why are you so angry?"

"Because luck didn't have anything to do with it. It was manipulation."

"Will you stop using that word! I didn't manipulate anybody into anything."

"Oh, but you did. You baited a trap and caught a prize fish. What about love?"

"Don't you worry about that! I will love my husband. I plan to love him plenty!"

"Plan! Ha! Love is not a plan. It's a happening that sneaks up on you before you know it. A feeling that grabs you like a vise. A desirable, all-consuming, exhilarating...excruciating. Painful." He stopped. Stared at her.

Damn! He was in love with her.

That's why he was acting like a damn fool. He was hurting. Sick. Mad with jealousy.

"I'm sorry," he whispered. "I...I don't know what got into me." He tried to smile.

She didn't say anything. She looked like she was trying to figure him out.

"Guess I panicked," he said. "The thought of losing the best assistant I ever had."

"It will leave you in a bit of a bind. Maybe we should start thinking about a replacement."

"No!" he said so vehemently that she started. "I...well, don't feel like dealing with it now. I've had one hell of a weekend. Bushed."

"I'm sorry. Shall I cover Fiscal this morning?"

"Please. And cancel Davis, will you? I think I'll call it a day."

"But..." She stopped, not wanting to say the day had just begun. He did look beat. "Why don't you do that? Nothing too pressing today."

He started out. Turned back. "Forget that bait stuff, will you?"

"Sure."

"And...be happy. Jake's a great guy."

"Thank you."

CHAPTER THIRTEEN

WHEN Clarice called that Wednesday morning, Lisa was in Scot's office, transferring material from her briefcase to his. The plan had been that she would accompany him to the meeting in Hawaii, but, at the last minute, he had changed his mind. "A routine meeting. Nothing major. I think I'd rather have you here."

Everything pretty routine here, also, she had thought, surprised. No pressures needing her attention at the office, and she had been looking forward to the trip. She had never been to Hawaii, and everyone said it was lovely. My, but she was getting spoiled! So, "Sure, boss. Whatever you say," had been her cheerful response.

"I'm putting the casualty stuff in," she said now. "But I don't think you need attend that session. As a matter of fact, it isn't necessary for—" His buzzer sounded.

She switched it on. "Yes?"

"It's for you, Lisa. A Mrs. Wells. She says it's urgent. Will you—?"

"Mary! Of course." She picked up the phone.

"Lisa!" It was Clarice. "I've got to talk to you."

"All right. But, could I call you back? I'm really rather—"

"It's about George," Clarice said. Lisa could tell she was crying. "He's...he's... I think he's seeing someone else."

Uh-oh! "Oh, I doubt that. We'll... Listen, I'll call you right back. I'm in the middle of something just now." She replaced the phone before Clarice could protest, and turned to Scot. "Sorry. My sister-in..." She stopped. Not her sister-in-law, but as good as. The Wells were as much her family as Aunt Ruth. "I mean, Clarice," she amended.

Not that it mattered. He wasn't listening. His eyes were focused on her, but it was as if they were looking through her at something else entirely. On his face that haggard expression it had worn all week. Which brought to mind what she was saying when Clarice interrupted.

"I think there are only one or two sessions which need your attention. Why don't you take it easy this trip? Go down to the beach and... Boss?"

"Oh. Sorry. What did you say?"

"I said you're due for a little R and R," she said, rather sternly. He really did need someone to look after him. "You've been going like a house afire. As a matter of fact, you could stay over for a few days. Lie on the beach, bask in the sun, swim in the ocean.''

''Sounds like a good idea.''

''You'll do it? Stay over, I mean?''

He shrugged. ''Why not?''

''Good. I'm going to change your reservations right now. Return flight next Tuesday. Okay?''

He nodded without enthusiasm.

''And don't you dare come back before then!'' She gave him a saucy grin and went into her own office.

Taking the sunshine with her, Scot thought, gazing after her.

Damn, but he was getting sentimental!

He was not a man given to sentimentality.

Nor was he one to brood over past mistakes. You win some, you lose some. Whichever...move on!

But this time... How the hell could it hurt so much to lose a game you weren't even playing?

That was it. He had never entered the arena. And why hadn't he? Why hadn't he realized she was the only woman he could ever love? So close to her for a whole year...no, three, if he counted the gopher years. Even then, as enchanted as he was by her lilting voice, her cheerful good nature, he hadn't known. Keen-sighted businessman he was, he'd just known she'd make a damn good assistant.

Even when he kissed her... Glands, she said, and he had bought it.

Glands, hell! He'd never been that turned on by just a kiss with any other woman.

Marriage bait. That had given him a laugh!

Well, sucker, the laugh's on you. You're caught in her trap as surely as Jake.

He pushed back his chair, got up and walked to the window. Stared out.

He didn't think much of marriage. In fact, had sworn off. But he knew that if she said the word, gave him half a chance, he'd have a ring on her finger and a halter around his neck just like that! Hell, he'd even retire if she required it. He wasn't as rich as Jake, but...

Ah, that was it. Jake.

Scot thrived on competition. It made the game more exciting. And for a prize he would cherish more than life itself...

But when the game was over, and the man holding the prize was his very best friend...

Damn. He'd have to start searching for a new assistant. It was dangerous to be around her at the office. Definitely no traveling with her.

Lisa and I together in Hawaii? Couldn't take the risk. Jake's too good a friend.

Lisa was not able to return Clarice's call until she got Scot off. By that time Clarice was almost hysterical and Lisa promised she would be there as soon as she could leave the office.

She drove over, wondering if George could really be involved with someone else. He and Clarice had been so close, since...goodness, since their early high school years. George, the big football hero, and Clarice, the beautiful. Popular, young, and healthy, with glands popping out all over the place. Glands which could often be mistaken for love.

Later?

Life, minus the cheering fans and the glamour, could become monotonous and dull. She knew that Clarice was unhappy and unfulfilled. Probably, so was George.

Yes, he could very well be involved with someone else. Probably, so would Clarice, if she could find the time. People should think with their heads about whom and what they wanted in a marriage before letting themselves be swept away by...well, face it...glands.

She thought of those two adorable children. What would happen to them if George and Clarice should break up? At the same time she was thinking, Nothing like that will ever happen to my children. Jake. He is everything I want. I'm glad I prepared myself to be the kind of wife he needs. I can make him happy. I'll give him my answer when he gets back from the golf match in Dover.

And why am I thinking of myself when I should be concentrating on Clarice? For the children's sake, she and George should stay together. Could this marriage be saved?

She parked her car in their driveway and walked rapidly toward the house.

"Lisa!" Betsy ran across the living room and flung herself into Lisa's arms, smearing something sticky all over her smart linen dress.

"Hello, pudding!" Lisa held her close. What were sticky hands against love? "I haven't seen you for so long. What's going on?"

"Daddy's not here, and Mommy's crying, and Todd won't stop sucking his thumb," said the little bundle of information.

So there. I shouldn't have asked. "Hello, Todd. How's my favorite boy?" Lisa set Betsy down and bent to tickle Todd, who was lying on the floor. He took his thumb out of his mouth long enough to giggle, but stuck it back in as Clarice pounced upon Lisa.

"You see!" she said, glancing accusingly at the clock. "It's after six and he's not here yet. Oh, Lisa, what am I to do?"

Clean up this mess for a start, was Lisa's first thought as she looked around for a safe place to deposit her shoulder bag. Finally she set it on top of two clean paperbacks on the coffee table, and said, "Why are you so concerned about time?

Traffic is so unpredictable and with that heavy rig he drives—''

"Oh, you don't know. He's a dispatcher now, with regular hours at the office here in town.''

"Good for him!" Lisa said, pleased. "No, I didn't know. That's a promotion, isn't it?"

"Oh, yes!" Clarice snorted. "Off every morning bright and early, dressed up in a coat and tie. Strutting like he's the head of the whole damn—''

"Clarice!" Lisa cut in. "We'll talk later," she said, with a significant glance toward Betsy, who watched them with big wide eyes and wide open ears. "After we bathe the kids. Have they eaten?"

"Oh, yes. Long ago. I've learned not to wait for George. He's never—''

"Clarice!"

"Oh, all right. But you don't know how it is." Clarice sounded like she was crying again, but she went into the bathroom and turned on the water.

"Come on, kids," Lisa said as she scooped Todd up. "Let's have a swim."

After a long bath and a couple of stories, the kids were settled in bed.

"It's driving me crazy," Clarice said as soon as they shut the bedroom door. "I don't even know who she is."

"You don't know if she is," Lisa said. "Come into the kitchen. I could use a cold drink. What does George say?"

"What could he say? You don't suppose he's going to tell me, do you? 'There's this gorgeous gal in the office and she asked me to stop by and fix a hinge on the door cabinet and I stayed for a drink and...'"

"What does he say?" Lisa demanded as she took down a pitcher and reached for the ice tea mix.

"That he's working, of course. An unexpected shipment or a truck stalled in Chicago. Work. What else?"

"Maybe he is working."

"Oh, no, he isn't. I know."

"How do you know?"

"Because even when he's here, he's not!" Clarice snapped.

"What do you mean by that?" Lisa asked as she filled two tall glasses with ice.

"I mean, he isn't... Doesn't... He just sleeps."

"Oh." Lisa handed her the glasses, picked up the pitcher of tea. "Let's go out on the patio."

"Oh, Lisa, what am I going to do?" Clarice asked again as soon as they were seated.

"Well," Lisa said. "If you're really convinced George is cheating on you, seems to me you have two choices. You can leave him, or—"

"Leave George? Never! Oh, Lisa, I couldn't live without George!" Clarice wailed and broke into almost uncontrollable sobs.

For a moment Lisa was too amazed to speak. Nothing about hating George, or what about the children and how would we manage. Just, "I couldn't live without George." She had been wrong. The only man Clarice would ever want to be involved with was George.

"If you can't live without him," she said, "then you must fight for him."

Clarice lifted a tear-stained face. "Oh, I couldn't do that. I could never confront George and demand—"

"I didn't say confront him. I said fight for him."

"How do I do that?"

"I've heard that the only way to compete with another woman is to make his time with you better and happier than his time with her. Make your place and yourself desirable and exciting."

Clarice shook her head. "That's all right for you. You have time to make yourself beautiful and desirable."

"Clarice! With all the time in the world I could never be as beautiful as you!"

Clarice's eyes brightened at the compliment. Then she sighed. "But I'm pretty dull, I guess. I don't have an exciting job or anything. Just feeding and diapering, and—"

"This is your job!" Suddenly Lisa was angry. "The most important job in the world. More exciting than being a homecoming queen. But not if you lie around on your butt eating chocolates all day. You have to work at it like any other job!" Lisa did lots of talking. Got Clarice's attention when she finished with, "if you don't want to live without George."

Still, she knew Clarice needed help. She spent two days with her, scrubbing, polishing, and bringing in flowers to "make sure you are the most desirable."

"It even smells pretty," Betsy announced, "and I'm not going to let Todd mess things up."

Lisa treated Clarice to a day at Hera's and shopped with her for "Sexy, stay-at-home clothes," she said, winking at Clarice. "Something Miss Other Woman can't wear at the office."

Late Saturday afternoon, she decided she had done all she could. They had made a start. The rest was up to Clarice, who was looking very pretty, very excited, and very determined. "Just be as sweet as you look, and everything is going to be all right," Lisa assured her, and believed that it would.

She had driven only two blocks when she saw George, in his blue Ford, heading home. She honked, attracting his attention. He was in this, too, she thought, and maybe a little talking would help. She parked and waited for George, who had parked on the other side, to come across the street.

"Well, if it isn't the beautiful boss lady herself!" he said, beaming at her. "Long way from those buck teeth, huh?"

"And you needn't remind me, George Wells."

"Just remembering you fondly," he said, laughing. "Don't see much of you these days, but Clarice keeps me informed. Do you just come visiting when I'm not at home?"

"Of course I visit when you're not there. Seems you never are."

"Oh. Clarice complaining?"

"Wouldn't you? What's going on, George?"

"Work. Been working from can to can't."

"Neglecting your family in the meantime?"

"Guess so . . . somewhat . . . I'm beat, Lisa. All I can do is hit the sack when I finally get home."

"Oh?"

He frowned. "I didn't want to tell Clarice. Wanted to surprise her. The house and the kids are getting too much for her, poor kid. And never a vacation. I've been working overtime as much as I could. Trying to raise a stake so I could take her to New York or Atlantic City for a little break. There's a good chance I'll get another promotion. Head dispatcher. Then I could hire a cleaning woman.''

"Oh, George, that's wonderful," Lisa said, feeling a surge of relief. "I mean, the promotions. You're really getting ahead. And you're right. Clarice could use a vacation.''

"Yeah, but maybe I should tell her why I'm working overtime.''

"No, don't. It would be such a nice surprise.'' A little worry won't hurt Clarice, she reasoned, and if it gives her a boost, so much the better. George needs some tender loving care. She grinned as she waved goodbye. He was in line for a surprise himself.

How wrong I was, she thought as she drove home. Those two were still madly in love with each other. So much in love that George was blind to a slovenly wife, a poorly kept house. All he could see was that Clarice was overloaded and needed a break. And Clarice, for all her complaints, knew with certainty that she "could not live without George.''

Glands. Maybe they were the determining factor. Or maybe it wasn't glands at all. But something deeper. Something that made one oblivious to altered appearances, imperfections, or faulty behavior.

But it went deeper than that. An exhilarating all-consuming feeling that made you know that this was the one man in all the world that you could not live without.

Did she feel like that about Jake?

She did not.

To marry him would be to cheat him.

CHAPTER FOURTEEN

JAKE had anchored the boat in a remote spot at a little island off the coast of Delaware. On the deck, he leaned against the rail and looked down at her. "So the answer is no? You won't marry me?"

She shook her head. "It wouldn't be fair. I don't... oh, Jake, I am fond of you. But it's not the love you deserve."

"I could wait."

"No. I... It won't change." She looked past him, at the trees and shrubbery, sea gulls fluttering over the blue waters. Perfect setting. Perfect man. She wished she did love him.

He touched her cheek. "Don't be sad, little one."

"I can't help it. I am sad, and ashamed. I shouldn't have pursued you."

"You! Sweetheart, it was the other way around. You don't even know how to pursue."

"Well, I tried. You see, I wanted to marry you because you're rich, and—"

"And you're one woman in a hundred who'd admit it. Oh, Lisa, Lisa!" He threw his arms around her and rocked back and forth, laughing. "No wonder I love you."

"Oh, stop it, Jake!" She hugged him back, and looked earnestly up at him. "It wasn't just because you're rich. You'd be a perfect husband."

"Oh? I've not been told that before. In fact, just the opposite. The consensus is that I'd be a terrible husband."

"Well, the consensus is wrong. You're good-natured, lovable, kind, generous, and fun to be with. All any woman could ask."

"Except you."

"Yes. I didn't have the good sense to fall in love with you. I'm sorry, but I hope ... we'll still be friends, won't we?"

"Of course. And you needn't be sorry. I'm disappointed. But not surprised."

"You're not?"

"No. I kept hoping, but I knew you didn't love me."

"How did you know?"

"Because I read you pretty well. Probably better than you read yourself."

"Oh? Between the lines, huh?"

"Pretty much. I'm more of an observer than I'm given credit for."

"And what do you observe about me?"

"That you're a planner. You've got the future script carefully written out, far in advance."

She wrinkled her nose, thinking about it.
"Okay. Maybe you're right. That's good, isn't
it?"

"Not for you. Your heart's too big."

"What do you mean by that?"

"Plans are thought out in your head. But your
heart doesn't think. It only feels. And your heart,
being the kind it is, sneaks in between the lines
of that carefully written script and blows all of
it to hell and back."

She didn't laugh. She simply stared at him.
"What are you really saying, Jake?"

"That maybe you're in love with someone
else."

That big heart he talked about...she felt it
swelling within her, almost choking her. "Why
do you say that?" she whispered.

"I've seen you look at him. Mind you, there
are only two occasions when I've been together
with the two of you. But both times it was for a
whole day. And, as I said, I'm a keen observer."

"I ..I don't want to be in love with...anyone
else " She didn't dare call his name. She didn't
have to

"Plans, huh?"

"Yes "

"Plans can get you in trouble."

She almost laughed. She had thought it was
glands   But that's just it. There are no plans in

that direction. Ours is purely a business relationship.''

"Oh, come off it, Lisa. That time in L.A. when I came in and kissed you, you shot a glance at him like you were asking his permission."

"It...it was just that I was surprised to see you, and—"

"Like hell it was. It burned me up!"

"You didn't act burned up."

"Ego, my dear. I don't easily admit defeat." He sighed. "I'm admitting it now. Tell me. Why are you resisting your heart?"

"I'm not."

"Are you denying that you love Scot?"

She couldn't deny it. "I told you we hardly see each other out of the office. We've never discussed—"

"Are you denying it?"

"Oh, why are you pressuring me?"

"Because Scot is the only man I'd want to have you if I can't."

"That's ridiculous. Scot isn't..."

"In love with you? Ha! He's so crazy about you he can't think straight."

She blinked. "You think..." Her voice trailed in the wonder, and hope flickered in her heart.

"It's just possible he loves you more than I."

She tried to absorb the feeling, the exhilaration. *He loves me. I didn't know, hadn't thought...* She had been too busy wrestling with her own feelings, trying to resist what now seemed too good to be true.

Jake gave a heavy sigh. "I wish you wouldn't look so delighted at this bit of news."

"Oh." She looked up at him, trying not to seem delighted. "It...it surprises me. Anyway, how can you know?"

"I know he almost hit me with his golf club when he thought I might be...er...trifling with your affections. And he really blew his top when I informed him that my intentions were honorable, that I was going to marry you."

"You told him that!"

He grinned. "Okay. So I lied. But I knew he wouldn't cut in on me if it were true. And, anyway, you hadn't said no. I was still hoping."

"Oh, Jake," was all she could say.

"All's fair in love, Lisa. Think about it. And think about where your heart is." He touched a gentle finger to her cheek. "Shall we sail down the coast a bit before we go back?"

He loves me, he loves me, he loves me. It was a song running through her mind, blocking out everything else.

Think about where your heart is, Jake had said. She couldn't stop thinking about it.

Her heart was with Scot, wherever he was, whatever he was doing. And her heart told her she wanted to be with him. Always and forever.

Her heart told her that she didn't care that he was a corporate ladder climber. To tell the truth, that was one of the things she liked about him. She was glad he was one of the movers and shakers that kept the economy going. Ambitious ladder climbers she had called them. True, many were ambitious just for themselves—Sam Elliot came to mind. But, whatever the ambition, they were all in there pitching, making a difference. In whatever field they worked, they were the ones building the economy, eliminating poverty throughout the world, weren't they? As important as anyone bent on building a marriage.

Marriage. She still wanted to marry, to have children, to stay at home with them.

But only if the marriage partner, the father, was Scot.

What did Scot Harding want?

She didn't know. How could she have worked so closely with him for three years and not know?

Because she had not wanted to know, to love him. She had thought of him as a business automaton.

How could she have thought that? When she had come to know him so well. She had observed his compassion with Jefrey. She had seen him at ease with Clarice's children. She had danced, had fun with him.

She had kissed him . . .

How had she not known that this was the man she could not live without?

And whatever he wanted, she wanted. If he were adverse to marriage ... If he wanted her to continue working as his assistant...

Yes, she would do that. Because she wanted to be always near him. And because he needed someone to care, to look after him.

He needed a wife.

Well, she was trained to be one, wasn't she!

She was like a cat on a hot tin roof as she awaited his return from Hawaii.

Jake said Scot loved her, didn't he?

Oh... what did Jake know?

The flight from Hawaii was boo-oo-ring. Nine hours to New York, and an hour on the company chopper to Wilmington. Driving home, he began to gather his thoughts for tomorrow.

He must get Miss Wilson, Lisa, out of his daily sight. The past few days had been real torture. She did her work okay, maybe even better, if that could be. But this absolute correctness of behavior was driving him up the wall. Particularly when he wanted her greater than sin. He'd not admitted it out loud—and wouldn't, certainly not now.

He should have replaced her when this thing began to get out of hand.

When was that?

Probably that first kiss. When he had come to her apartment. Those kids were there and both she and the place had looked a mess. But she had had the business together, and he... It had been a light, simple congratulatory kiss. But it had jolted the hell out of him. He had ignored it. The other times...

Oh, hell! He'd replace her tomorrow... first thing.

She would fit nicely in the satellite office in New Haven. He seldom had to go there. If he did, he'd make sure it was after she had retired to the lap of luxury with Jake. He wondered how soon that would be.

When he got to the office next morning, Lisa was, as usual already in place.

"Good morning, Mr. Harding," came the cheerful intonation. "I've changed the blend this morning. I hope you like it. It's Mocha Supreme."

"Okay. I probably will," he said rather absently, his mind rehearsing what he had to say. "Lisa, would you please sit down."

She sat, looking at him in a strange way. Studying his face as if to find... what? It made him nervous.

He cleared his throat. "I've pondered the matter of your career development."

"My career development!"

"Why...er...yes." Why did she look like he had slapped her face? Her expression, the way she kept staring at him... He felt even more uncomfortable and began to speak rapidly. "You are familiar with our satellite office. You know, the Think Tank in New Haven?"

Lisa nodded, but her eyes still held his. Like someone waiting for a shoe to drop.

He cleared his throat again, and tried to keep his voice steady.

"Mr. Cummings, VP for R. and D., has for a long time had need of a Chief of Staff. In fact, he's asked about your availability some time back. But I thought you might not wish to change your agenda then. But now...well, things are different."

"Different? You're trying to get rid of me?"

"Yes. That is... No!" He blundered on. "You've been a top-notch assistant to me. And you deserve to move up. Moreover, this will be a substantial salary increase, and... Why are you staring at me like that?"

"I'm trying to see if what Jake said is true."

Jake. "Right. Salary increase...a joke," he said, sending a pencil spinning across his desk. "As if money will have any effect in your new station. Nor would you, I suppose, be interested in any job."

"Aren't you interested in what Jake said?"

"Not particularly."

"It interested me. He said you love me."

Damn him. "He didn't have to rub it in."

"Do you love me?"

He sighed, nodded. "Yes. That's why I thought... Darn it, Lisa. It's difficult to... Well, it's better you work somewhere else until you marry. When, by the way, is the great event coming off?"

"You haven't asked."

For a full minute he couldn't speak. She was smiling, a tender smile that touched his heart, turned his despair into hope. "Jake?" he managed.

"Doesn't feel inclined to marry a woman who is madly in love with someone else." Now there was no mistaking the message in her eyes.

"Lisa! Oh, Lisa!" His chair slammed back. He was on his feet, reaching for her. In a moment she was in his arms, and he was kissing her, drinking in the sweet precious essence of her love. Feeling the kindle of desire, the vibrations of passion surge through him. Reveling in the relief, the joy that she was his. "I've been through pure hell, loving you so much."

"And never showing it," she said. "You never once said you loved me."

"Didn't know. You said it was glands," he teased, his lips nuzzling her ear.

Her soft moan told him her desire equalled his, but when at last she spoke, she sounded wary.

"Oh, Scot, maybe it is...just glands, I mean." She looked earnestly up at him. "I only know that when you touch me or just look at me in a certain way I go all hollow and eager inside."

"Keep feeling that way, love."

"But it's almost..." She hesitated and he looked down to see that she was actually blushing. "Oh, I want you so much that nothing else in the whole world matters."

This was his Lisa, direct and blatantly honest. He smiled.

"It's shameful." She sighed and lay her head on his shoulder. "But it's true. I only want to be with you. I certainly don't want any promotion or any other job. I'll keep working as your assistant since you're against marriage."

"I never said anything like that," he said, quite shocked. It was true that he had been somewhat against marriage, but he'd never said so to her, had he?

"Well, you said I was silly to call it an occupation and plot and plan to—" His buzzer interrupted and she switched it on. "Yes, Celes?"

Scot cut in. "Hold all calls, Celes. I'm in the middle of something." He switched off the buzzer and turned to Lisa. "I'm planning the most important phase of my life. Marriage to the only woman I could ever love."

"You're sure?"

"You don't think I'd waste all your careful preparation, do you?"

"Children and all?"

"Children and all. What does your book say about rushed wedding plans?"

"Oh, Scot, I do love you. And I promise I'll be the best wife ever. I won't even complain when you have to make those long trips."

"You won't have to. I've moved up the corporate ladder. While in Hawaii, I was called and informed that I had been elected Chairman of the Board. So now I'll have a lovely bride that will make the members more comfortable. Protocol almost insists that the board prexy be accompanied by his wife when travel is required."

"President!" Lisa beamed. "Oh, Scot, that's wonderful. You'll be perfect. I can see you, your eyes on the smallest detail while keeping track of the largest project. And with your clear thinking and honest approach, your compassion and concern for everyone. Oh, there are so many things I love about you, Scot. It's not just glands."

"That's good to know. But, meanwhile..." A wry smile twisted his lips as he pulled her into his arms. "Let's check the glands."

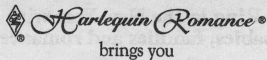
Harlequin Romance ®
brings you

SIMPLY THE BEST

Authors you'll treasure, books you'll want to keep!

Harlequin Romance books just keep getting better and better…and we're delighted to welcome you to our Simply the Best showcase for 1997.

Each month for a whole year we'll be highlighting a particular author—one we know you're going to love!

Watch for:

#3445 _MARRY ME_
by Heather Allison

TV presenter Alicia Hartson is a romantic: she believes in Cupid, champagne and roses, and Mr. Right. Tony Domenico is not Mr. Right! He's cynical, demanding and unromantic. Where Alicia sees happy endings, her boss sees ratings. But they do say that opposites attract, and it is Valentine's Day!

Available in February wherever
Harlequin books are sold.

Look us up on-line at: http://www.romance.net

BEST2

Ring in the New Year with babies, families and romance!

NEW YEAR'S RESOLUTION:

Add a dash of romance to your
holiday celebrations with this
delightful, heartwarming collection
from three outstanding romance
authors—bestselling author
JoAnn Ross
and
award winners
Anne Stuart and **Margot Dalton.**

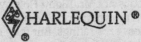

HARLEQUIN ®

Look us up on-line at: http://www.romance.net

NYRB

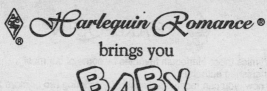

Harlequin Romance ®

brings you

BABY BOOM

We are proud to announce the birth of our
new bouncing baby series—Baby Boom!

Each month in 1997 we'll be bringing you your very
own bundle of joy—a cute, delightful romance by one
of your favorite authors. Our heroes and heroines are
about to discover that two's company and three (or
four…or five) is a family!

This exciting new series is all about the true labor
of love…

Parenthood, and how to survive it!

Watch for:
#3443 *THREE LITTLE MIRACLES*
by Rebecca Winters

Tracey couldn't forget the devastating secret that had forced her
to run out on Julien Chappelle four days after their honeymoon.
What she hadn't counted on was that her brief marriage had left
more than memories. A set of adorable triplets who needed
their mom to come home! It seemed Tracey had only one
motive for leaving, and three reasons to stay….

Available in February wherever
Harlequin books are sold.

Look us up on-line at: http://www.romance.net   BABYB2

HARLEQUIN®

Don't miss these Harlequin favorites by some of our most distinguished authors!
And now, you can receive a discount by ordering two or more titles!

HT#25645	THREE GROOMS AND A WIFE by JoAnn Ross	$3.25 U.S. $3.75 CAN.	☐
HT#25647	NOT THIS GUY by Glenda Sanders	$3.25 U.S. $3.75 CAN.	☐
HP#11725	THE WRONG KIND OF WIFE by Roberta Leigh	$3.25 U.S. $3.75 CAN.	☐
HP#11755	TIGER EYES by Robyn Donald	$3.25 U.S. $3.75 CAN.	☐
HR#03416	A WIFE IN WAITING by Jessica Steele	$3.25 U.S. $3.75 CAN.	☐
HR#03419	KIT AND THE COWBOY by Rebecca Winters	$3.25 U.S. $3.75 CAN.	☐
HS#70622	KIM & THE COWBOY by Margot Dalton	$3.50 U.S. $3.99 CAN.	☐
HS#70642	MONDAY'S CHILD by Janice Kaiser	$3.75 U.S. $4.25 CAN.	☐
HI#22342	BABY VS. THE BAR by M.J. Rodgers	$3.50 U.S. $3.99 CAN.	☐
HI#22382	SEE ME IN YOUR DREAMS by Patricia Rosemoor	$3.75 U.S. $4.25 CAN.	☐
HAR#16538	KISSED BY THE SEA by Rebecca Flanders	$3.50 U.S. $3.99 CAN.	☐
HAR#16603	MOMMY ON BOARD by Muriel Jensen	$3.50 U.S. $3.99 CAN.	☐
HH#28885	DESERT ROGUE by Erine Yorke	$4.50 U.S. $4.99 CAN.	☐
HH#28911	THE NORMAN'S HEART by Margaret Moore	$4.50 U.S. $4.99 CAN.	☐

(limited quantities available on certain titles)

	AMOUNT	$
DEDUCT:	**10% DISCOUNT FOR 2+ BOOKS**	$
ADD:	**POSTAGE & HANDLING**	$
	($1.00 for one book, 50¢ for each additional)	
	APPLICABLE TAXES*	$_____
	TOTAL PAYABLE	$_____
	(check or money order—please do not send cash)	

To order, complete this form and send it, along with a check or money order for the total above, payable to Harlequin Books, to: **In the U.S.:** 3010 Walden Avenue, P.O. Box 9047, Buffalo, NY 14269-9047; **In Canada:** P.O. Box 613, Fort Erie, Ontario, L2A 5X3.

Name:_____
Address:_____ City:_____
State/Prov.:_____ Zip/Postal Code:_____

*New York residents remit applicable sales taxes.
Canadian residents remit applicable GST and provincial taxes.
Look us up on-line at: http://www.romance.net

HBACK-JM4